To Helen

The star that guides my ship

SOUL BAY PRESS LTD
SUSSEX
Soul Bay Press Limited
3rd Floor Map House
34-36 St Leonards Road
Eastbourne
East Sussex
BN21 3UT

Registered in England No: 06322122

Registered office as above

1st Edition - Published in 2012

Design by Dan Conway & Alan Stepney
Typeset by Alan Stepney
in Times New Roman
Soul Bay Press Logo © Alan Stepney & APF

Printed and bound in the United Kingdom by
CPI Group (UK) Ltd, Croydon, CR0 4YY
A CIP catalogue for this book is available from the British Library

ISBN 978-0-9559553-8-9

ACKNOWLEDGEMENTS

Enormous thanks to Andy Franks for asking me to write this book and for publishing it. Thanks also to the rest of the team at Soul Bay Press: Daniel Conway, Samantha Herron and Tom Jenkins. Special mention must be made of Alan Stepney for his fantastic art direction and the effort he put into forging an unruly manuscript into a book.

Helen, George and Daniel - my constellation, love to you all.

A NEW SCIENCE OF NAVIGATION

by

Martin Jenkins

To which is added:

A Capital Grimoire
Last Exclamations of Sufferers
The Dreadful DEADMAN
& etcetera.

All of which serve to tell of the Many
forthcoming Mutations of this City:
a Prophecie.

All of especial concernment of these Times.

As also most compassionately informing, and
most lovingly and pathetically advising and
warning LONDON.

With Hints to the deciphering of the *Darke
Hieroglyphs* of the World's Purpose.

Believe it, you fuckers -
***Especially* you high and mighty bastards.**

LONDON,
Imprinted for S... B.. P...., and are to be sold at the
Cock in Ludgate-street, and at the *Castle* in Cornhill.

mmxii

My Deare One.

All or None.

Everyone under the Sunne:

overturn, overturn, overturn

quickly, quickly,
now, now

London's Burning, London's Burning,
            Fetch the Engines, Fetch the Engines,
                Fire, Fire; Fire, Fire

        (in catch or round, altogether now)

                        a new Hierusalem

'We were in Clerkenwell I think, a cold autumn night. Priesty John tottered out of the pub after us. We were all having a fag in a huddle against the cold; Priesty John entered our circle with its rising ring of smoke. There was a half-hearted fog roiling over the roads slick with the recent rain. The street lights orange-yellow: everything glistening. Priesty John looked a bit wobbly; amphetamine-thin in a grotty old greatcoat. He held a single-strand rollie in his shaking hands, a box of matches in the other. He cleared his throat noisily, shifting a recalcitrant bolus of phlegm. Done, he uttered:

"Y'know, there's an old legend that when God created man he took different coloured earth from all over the world, blended it all together and made us in his likeness."

He paused. We waited, shivering.

"That's shite." he continued. "Man was made from London Clay."

Priesty John looked down with rheumy eyes at his roll-up, shook his head slowly and shuffled back into the pub. There was a brief flash of light, a blast of warm, beery air and the hubbub of voices - then the door swung shut.

We stood silently drawing on our cigarettes and then, flicking the butts into the gutter, we followed him in. A constellation of glasses waited for us on our table.'

A tatty parade of shops on a stretch of Green Lanes as it edges beyond Wood Green, yearning towards the North Circular and the sunnier, boskier climes of Palmers Green.

It was a pleasant sunny morning and there was a fair old hubbub on the pavements.

Next to the minicab office there was a door that led to stairs straight up to the rooms above. A hand-written card was pinned to the door jamb next to the bell.

Denys Wilson

Psychic Tarot Cards Spells

Judith - Horoscopes

10am - 5pm Ring and Come Up!

The card was curling and yellowed, the black biro had faded almost to nothing.

Two schoolboys dawdled along the pavement. Huge knots on ties at half mast.

One stopped and nudged the other, pointing at the notice. He took his permanent marker (always at hand for impromptu tagging) from his blazer pocket: he *was* going to write SEXY MODEL but at the last moment he was prompted to scrawl: PRIVATE DETECTIVE beneath the top name. The boy stepped back to survey his work and shrugged: not that funny...but, well, fuck it...

They resumed their promenade.

'No supernatural claims are made for this air freshener.'

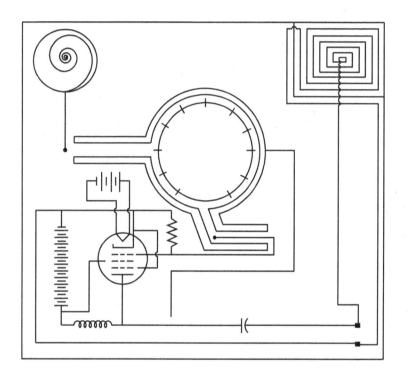

The machine is operating...

The machine is operating ...more or less.

Consider…

Desire…

Sidereal: of the stars.

dark sun - dark moon - shadow planets - dark matter - dark life.

Underworld, Underground - 'All change!'

The crystals are magnetized - place the glowing green radio snow in the hopper.

Cat's whisker to the crystal.

Duchamp says that the sexual act is *the pre-eminent fourth dimensional situation'* so get fucking.

NORTH

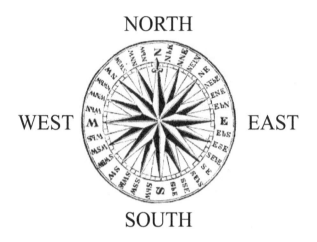

WEST   EAST

SOUTH

Mnemonic: Never Eat Sea Weed

A NEW SCIENCE OF NAVIGATION

'In science there are no 'depths';
                            there is surface everywhere...'
The Scientific Conception of the World, Der Wiener Kreis

'...time and space are an intellectual hoax...'
                                        Mina Loy

'Existence is percipi or percipere. The horse is in the stable,
the Books are in the study as before.'
                                        George Berkeley

'Who knows whether, in nature, we do not occupy just as
small a place alongside beings whose existence we do not
suspect as our cats and dogs that live with us in our homes?'
                                        William James

100010100100010101011101010100010100100
010101011101010100010100100010101011101
010100010100100010101011101010100010100
100010101011101010100010100100010101011
101010100010100100010101011101010100010
100100010101011101010100010100100010101
011101010100010100100010101011101010100
010100100010101011101010100010100100010
101011101010100010100100010101011101010
100010100100010101011101010100010100100
010101011101010100010100100010101011101
010100010100100010101011101010100010100
100010101011101010100010100100010101011
101010100010100100010101011101010100010
100100010101011101010100010100100010101
011101010100010100100010101011101010100
010100100010101011101010100010100100010
101011101010100010100100010101011101010
100010100100010001010010001010101110101
010001010010001000101001000101010111010
101000101001000101001000101010111010101
000101001000101010111010101000101001000
010001010101110101010001010010001010101
110101010001010010001010101110101010001
001010101110101010001010010001010101110
101010111010101000101001000101010111010
100010100100010101011101010100010100100
010101011101010100010100100010001010010
001010101110101010001010010001010101110
1010100010101001000100010001000100 scrap of
sailcloth - diode - pitch and wax - myrhh
- copperwire 010010100010010001000 0110
100010100100010101011101010100010100100
010101011101010100010100100010101011101
010100010100100010101011101010100010100
010001010101110101010001010010001010101
110101010001010010001010101110101010000
101001000101010111010101000101001000101
010111010101000110100100010101011101010

$$J_i = \frac{dn_i/dt}{S_p} = -D_i \left(\frac{dc_i(x)}{dx} - c_i(x) \frac{z_i F}{R T} \frac{d\psi(x)}{dx} \right)$$

Night. A block of flats in north London: white concrete and glass. Zoom in on the top flat:

Mad Scientist vibe on this one: a man in a white coat, wild hair and eyes, the works. A pneumatic blond assistant decked out in an Ann Summers' Naughty Nurse uniform. White rubber tunic and opaque white stockings with satin bow tops. A range of sexy accessories including stethoscope, elbow length gloves and a nurse's hat. With eyes wide she brings her hands to her mouth and thrills a scream: a cackling hunchback pulls a lever.

BIG SCIENCE CUNNING MAN.

The Scientist calibrates Hieronymus readings with the Lethbridge Scale. The scene is lit by the globes of a Van der Graff generator which crackle and spark, reek of ozone.

The assistant's dress rides up exposing her stocking tops, her tits are spilling from the unbuttoned top - the Mad Scientist disentangles a hard-on from his corduroy trousers and pulls her panties down. She's wet and ready; he enters her quickly and fucks frenziedly: he comes screaming 'Method, we believe in you!'

Big spark - shrack! Smell of electrical discharge in the air, vacuum tubes and flickering lights, Tesla coils and Van der Graaf generators, a Jacob's ladder.

The Scientist and his assistant subside. The hunchback relaxes: he pulls off his costume and removes the hump improvised from a pillow.

The ritual is over.

Half-lives and spectral analyses.

Ghosting in on the moderne: no gothic pile but a Corbusier-style villa WITH GHOSTS.

Initial data:

First communication: 'We are trying to get through…'

Manners here among the whispering dead.

Sterile conversation between a dead man and a man living on borrowed time.

Surfing surface; glitter of light on water; experimental METHOD.

Alchemy of the word.

'Method! we believe in you...'

We are already elsewhere…

Denys awoke. Judith had got up earlier and left. Dry mouth. Stab of a headache in the right temple and eye. Slight nausea. Aching kidneys. Too much to drink again. It would all come together. Be patient.

Denys swung his legs out of the bed and sat for a moment before tentatively standing. He felt a bit wobbly. He lit a cigarette and rode the first hit of the smoke as he went to the bathroom. He balanced the cigarette on the edge of the sink while he quickly brushed his teeth and splashed water on his face.

Denys briefly considered putting on a suit but he had never quite got the knack of wearing a suit; they always looked as if they wanted to be elsewhere and were just hanging around waiting for a better offer. He had a white linen suit that looked fantastic - until he put it on. The suit would crumple around him, stains blossomed, an unaccountable stench of sweat, fags and booze: suddenly he was Denholm Elliott playing a gin-soaked colonial in the Far East. He opted for jeans and a t-shirt.

Out into the north London residential street. He would have breakfast at Chris the Greeks caff. He made his way unsteadily down the street. A neighbour gave him a nod of recognition. Collapse of the wave function: Denys was sure now he existed. *Esse est percipi.*

Everything was going too fast. Denys breathed in and out, deeply and slowly.

It was a blue sky early summer day, pleasantly warm. As Denys was passing the local mini-mart he saw the Lily White Boys standing under the bus shelter. The Lily White Boys were a local fixture. Sta-prest and Fred Perry in greys and blues, pork pie hats. They were slim, sad-eyed and soulful. They were finger-clicking and singing harmonies.

It was presumed by most locals that the Lily White Boys were brothers; others said they were in fact sisters, drag kings. Or boy and girl. Not related but lovers. Related and lovers. Judith said they were the living embodiment of Gemini, sign of London.

Denys hurried on.

And now the Shipping Forecast, issued by the Met Office at 06.00 GMT today.

The are warnings of gales in Barnet, Chigwell and Kingston-upon Thames.

The general synopsis: Low, Hammersmith, 978, deepening rapidly. Expected Theydon Bois, 964, by noon today. Hyperborean gods of fire, ice and iron rising.

Ealing: Northeast 3 or 4, occasionally 5 later. Occasional rain. Moderate or poor.

Westminster: East 4. Grinding of dark satanic mills expected. Poor.

Camden Town: Southwest 4 or 5. Squally showers. Good becoming moderate in showers. Moderate icing.

Mitcham: North 7. Gusting. Signs and wonders expected. Moderate.

Rainham Marshes: East 3. Unquiet dead looming towards dusk. Poor.

City of London: North or northeasterly 5. Continues besieged by the dispossessed. Good.

The average temperature will be hovering about three degrees above absolute zero so best wrap up well and tune in to zero-point quantum energy.

Microsleep.

Capital is an out of control, would-be god called Mammon (the real Mammon has retired and lives in a bed-sit in West Hampstead): converting analogue persons (many non-human) to digital bits, negating the agency and will of all persons; black hole of neither life nor death, everywhere and nowhere.

Capital/Mammon is due to disappear up his own arse soon taking the lot of us with him unless he is busted down to size. Mammon skulks off, broken, a whining little ghost. 'Not fair, not fair...'. Fuck off to some graveyard and try and frighten the kids.

Battlelines cut across everyday life. Weapons of the poets. Finding the symbolic sweet spot, the weakest link in the semiotic chain. The poets and sorcerers of the world disdain to conceal their views....a spectre is haunting...

The best symbol for a sharp sword is a sharp sword. Invoke the Great Transparents: they work by mimicry not identity *and so should we*. Demand the *bona fides* of these so-called gods, entities, enlightened beings and their piss-poor parish pump gurus. Join us in a hypercosmic communism or FUCK OFF. Enough of this 'mood music' from elsewhere, 'gotta get the people on board with the right narrative'. Endless reiteration of tired topologies and typologies, mired in illusory space and time. Policy wonks of the astral plane; ghostly spin doctors; Circumlocution Office of the Other World. What did Priesty John say? 'No more stories, never again.'

The best symbol for a sharp sword is *not* a sharp sword.

Winchmore Hill: the middle classes go about their business, carrying take-out coffees, criss-crossing the Green. Blue skies and sunshine but there is still a hint of early morning chill in the air. The flower shop: *Belladonna*. Outside the shop, two chairs: on them sat Richard 'Don't call me Dick' Hay, sole prop. and Paul Ferguson, struggling thespian. It was early but they had already taken the top off a bottle of vile grappa and were sipping it, wincing with each sip. They were having a good old bitch.

Richard had had a brief career as a celebrity florist. *Enfant terrible* of the 2003 RHS Chelsea Young Florist of the Year competition: a single white orchid on a slab of bloodied horsemeat. Breakfast TV, his own show, briefly, on some also-ran lifestyle channel and tabloid tittle-tattle about his serial womanising with z-list babes. Vodka and cocaine. Just the shop now and fading recognisability. He was thinning out, ceasing to exist.

Paul has problems too and was holding forth in his fruity actor's voice, slightly too loud:

'…so it was meant to be a big costume drama. Conrad - very literary. *Under Western Eyes*. I went along for the launch… some shithole in Soho…they'd fucked up on the budget and got some dodgy gangsters in to to stump up the final cash. They'd asked for 'changes'. So, they ran the fucking show reel and they'd only cut in loads of porn scenes. I was livid. Devastated. "I don't know what you're complaining about," the director said, "your body-double's got a big knob." Jesus H. Christ and all the saints! They'd renamed it *Under Western Thighs*. I was totally pissed on comp brandy by the time we did our stuff for the press and I passed out into the ample *décolletage* of Miss C. L. O'Hara, porn starlet *de jour*. An explosion of flashbulbs and bingo! it's all over the redtops. Anyway, seems like I'm contracted for another one. Can't wriggle out of it. "It's all work, darling." my agent says. Lazy cunt. It's another porn Conrad: *Arse of Darkness.* There's already talk of following that one up with *Lord Jism.*'

Richard made half-hearted noises of sympathy. He's been there.

Denys trundled up. 'Hiya, Dic…Richard. Bit early for an *aperitif* isn't it.'

'Probably. Want one?'

'Yeah.'

Richard went inside and reappeared with a smeared glass and filled it. Denys took a sip and grimaced.

'Fuck.'

Richard introduced Denys and Paul.

'Sorry, got to hurry. Have you got the stuff in I wanted?' Denys asked. He didn't want to get caught in lost hours of alcohol and bitterness: there was time enough for that later.

Richard got in various botanicals that Denys needed in return for the occasional card-reading or death spell. He made vague claims to being 'spiritual' but seemed driven by petty jealousy and the memory of ancient, largely imaginary wrongs.

'Yeah, no worries…come inside.'

Denys emptied his glass and followed.

They went into the shop. It was large and neat. White tiles and cool green light - silvered pots and vivid flowers of red,

31

yellow and orange. There was a door behind the counter that led upstairs to Richard's flat; another door at the back of the shop was ajar and Richard's garden could be seen beyond. It was his secret joy: there he grew belladonna and passion flower, hemlock and monkshood, oleander and Lily of the valley. All poisonous, deadly. Moonseed from which curare is distilled, larkspur, milkweed and many others flourished under his green fingers.

Richard dreamed fondly of collectively offing the Steering Committee of the British Floristry Society.

Richard looked behind the counter and found the goods. Denys put his glass down on the counter and took the three proffered polybags of dried plants. The bags had white labels with handwritten scrawls: Cascara Sagrada, Mugwort, Orris Root.

'Brilliant. I owe you one. Gotta shoot.' Denys said.

He made off as Richard resumed his interrupted conversation:

'The fucking tele AND radio have gone crazy…they won't work right…'

Denys decided to cut across the churchyard. and surreptitiously scoop up some graveyard earth. More vital supplies.

Sorted.

The office on Green Lanes. The altered card was still pinned to the door jamb. The street door had been left open. At the top of the stairs another door had also been left ajar more in hope than expectation, leading to an office. The office smelled of cheap coffee, cheaper fags and a dozen rarer incenses, faint exotic traces of sandlewood, frankincense, myrhh and many others. Sudden vistas of...elsewhere.

The daylight had made a valiant attempt to penetrate the flyblown windows and, exhausted, failed - the room looks as faded as the card below except for another door painted a garish and unwise shade of orange. In this subdued setting the door would be grounds for a charge of common assault. The door itself has evidently made it's own decision and is shedding the paint in great flakes, bright flecks ground into the threadbare carpet of indeterminate pattern.

A desk, a phone and a filing cabinet. On the desk was a litter of small, stubby lager bottles and an overflowing ashtray. A copy of last years *Old Moore's Almanac*. A deck of worn tarot cards. A spread of ordinary playing cards fills the space that remains.

A tea tray ('Scenes of Kent') on top of the filing cabinet had stubs of different coloured candles on it rising from a psychedelic mess of wax.

Beyond the orange door Denys Wilson, Psychic, sat slumped in an ancient leather armchair reading a book. Denys's relation to the chair was the same as that of a hermit crab to its shell; full symbiosis cannot be far off.

Denys was in his mid-forties and his perpetual lager and ciarette diet that had stood him in such good stead since his teenage years had stopped working - the image of the Clash's 'London Calling' album cover on his t-shirt had a definite fisheye lens effect and his jeans were not worn low as a fashion statement.

Judith Kitson paced around the room. If the outer office was faded, this room ('the staff room' Denys called it) was positively stygian in it's gloom. She was both Denys' business and romantic partner: on both counts she was unsure why.

Judith made her way to the window and lifted a slat of the Venetian blind and gazed vacantly out. Two old blokes had spilled out from the Turkish drinking club opposite and were duelling with pool cues in slow motion. It was strictly handbags at dawn and Judith barely registered them. Next to the drinking club was a Spiritualist Church - their 'loyal opposition'. Old women would climb the stairs and Judith would draw up a 'spook chart' or Denys would read the cards for them, rehearsing the questions they would later ask again over the road. Departed husbands, family members taken untimely.

'Pull up the blinds, why don't you?' said Denys.

'Dunno...makes me feel like a detective, looking out like this. It's a stakeout.' Judith replied brushing back black hair from her pale face.

She was slim and attractive; tight jeans, tight t-shirt. Though only a couple of years younger than Denys she had worn far better.

'That's odd....I felt a bit detective-y this morning. Picked this up before I left home.' Denys replied. He held up a tattered old paperback of *'The Saint in London'* by Leslie Charteris.

Though they were a couple Judith still had her own place ten minutes or so from Denys' flat. On any given day Denys was never sure if they would be sleeping together that night: he respected her desire to have her 'own space' and he found it frustrating as hell. She had stayed at her own flat the previous night and Denys still carried her absence then with him now.

Denys went back to his book for a few minutes while Judith continued to gaze out onto the street.

'We need some cash.' Denys suddenly announced to the world in general. The sudden breaking of the silence seemed to surprise them both.

'Yeah, well, I know that...'

'You've got...what...two horoscope readings booked today? I've got one card reading and I might be able to flog a planetary talisman to one of your punters if we're lucky. Maybe one or two walk-ins at best.'

'It's been busier.' Judith agreed.

'So, d'you want to do some sex magick?'

Judith gives a small *moue* of disgust: 'Not especially. No. What for?'

'Sex magick. For cash.'

'What, you pay me for sex?'

'Come on. To magic up some readies...conjure some moolah.' Denys said irritably, rubbing his thumb and forefinger together.

'Can't you do a candle spell or something?'

Denys gestured towards an old, low table. Their money tree was brown, shrivelled and dry - it had incontrovertibly died in it's pot. The tall glass jar with *Money Spell* and dollar signs screenprinted in white on it was empty save for the stub of green candle that had guttered out at the bottom.

'Nah! Come on - we always get good results this way.'

Denys was wheedling now; suddenly desperate and horny.

'And it's fun!'

Judith shot him a look of utter incredulity.

'Don't be like that, babe.' Denys said, trying to sound and look hurt.

Judith looked with distaste at Denys who seemed to be visibly receding into the armchair. She sighed: 'O.K.'

Still seated Denys started to unbuckle his belt. Judith gave an involuntary shudder of horror: the very armchair seemed to be quivering with anticipation.

'Oh Christ, at least wash your knob first, wont you?'

Not caring to contest the implication of his unsavoury demeanour Denys disappeared into the tiny toilet and mercifully closed the door. Sound of running water. A minute or so later he reappeared, belt undone, fly open. Drops of water have spattered his jeans which were already tented by a bulge.

Denys went off into the office. His trousers held precariously in place only by his hips, causing him to move with a curious legs akimbo waddle. He rifled impatiently through the desk drawers with much muttering and eventually extricated a small folded piece of parchment.

'Got you, my little beauty.' he exclaimed giving the paper

a little kiss before making his awkward progress back to the other room.

Standing in front of the armchair Denys unceremoniously pulled his trousers and boxers down: his thickened cock stood at twenty five to twelve. He subsided into the armchair's welcoming embrace.

Judith came and stood in front of Denys. Hands on hips she looked down at him with a mixture of fond amusement and sorrow.

'Aren't you going to get your kit off?' Denys asked thoughtfully.

'No.'

'At least get your tits out.'

Sighing again Judith quickly pulled her 'Hello Kitty' t-shirt over her head and dropped it onto the floor. She unclipped her bra and dropped it on top of the t-shirt.

Denys gave a low whistle of appreciation.

They were nice tits. His cock rose to twenty to twelve. He took a sly peek hoping to see the delicate rose bloom of arousal on Judith's breasts and neck but it was absent.

'Oh, well,' he thought, 'this *is* work.'

He unfolded the parchment and stared with intense concentration. The pattern on the paper was as tangled and cryptic as that on the office carpet. It was his 'Money Now' sigil. He tried to tune Judith out and meditate solely on the sigil but...well, a blow job is a blow job.

Judith got on her knees and started playing with his prick. It stiffened rapidly through the quarter to ten to twelve. She lowered her head and took his cock in her mouth.

Denys continued to stare at the sigil; his eyes were glazed and his breath came faster and deeper as Judith's head bobbed up and down.

It didn't take long. Twelve struck early. The sigil was charged.

Denys pulled up his boxers leaving his jeans round his ankles. He'd get back to them later. He looked more vacant than usual. The armchair looked set to swallow him more completely than Judith had done.

There was a sound of feet on the stairs and then a man's voice calling.

'Hello? Hello?....Shop!'

'Bingo!' Denys exclaimed, suddenly galvanised. 'That was quick.'

Judith didn't hear - she was already in the bathroom looking for the mouthwash.

Denys stood up abruptly and almost fell flat on his face but he recovered himself. He pulled up his trousers. He was still rethreading his belt as he entered the front office.

A portly middle aged man in a navy blue raincoat was flapping his arms and looking around in a bemused fashion.

'Ah...hello.' he said.

'Hi. I'm Denys Wilson. How can I help?'

The man caught sight of the still topless Judith in the room beyond as she came out of the bathroom. She gave a delicate ladylike 'eek!' and rapidly crossed her arms across her chest. Ignoring her and the man's goggle eyed stare Denys deftly kicked the door behind shut with his heel.

Denys grinned like an idiot as the visitor crimsoned in

embarrassment.

'Maybe I should...um...come back later?'

'No!' Denys cried with an edge of desperation in his voice. The man looked decidedly well-heeled. Denys took possession of himself.

'No. Not at all.' he said smoothly. 'My...colleague is... just...um...spot of staff training.'

The man looked distinctly ill at ease and plucked at a shirt collar that looks a few sizes too small for his pudgy neck.

'NVQ.' Denys continued by way of continuing unconvincing explanation.

'I heard that!' Judith shouted through a tangled t-shirt from the room beyond. Then quieter but quite distinctly she mutters: 'Wanker!'

The man chose not to hear the comment.

'You're a detective...a private detective? I saw the notice downstairs.' he said.

Denys blinked in momentary befuddlement and then recovered.

'Umm...I can be...yes. I mean, I am. Our methods are... er...unorthodox but we always get our man.' Denys said smoothly. 'What's the case?'

The man handed Denys a buff file and his card. A name, Mr Malcolm Barrow and a mobile number. No job description, nothing else.

'My employer would like you to track down the person in this file. A relative. Discretion is expected but I am sure that goes without saying.'

'Right. Yes.' Denys blustered, clutching the file like a

drowning man holding on to driftwood. 'We charge £300 *per diem* plus expenses. A cheque and maybe a small cash advance as a retainer.'

'Absolutely.' the man replied. He took his wallet from his jacket and slid out some crisp new £50 note. Denys's eyes lit up.

'Will £300 be ok?' I can get a cheque sent over this afternoon; a weeks worth, say?'

Denys looked at proffered cash in the man's hands blankly.

'Yes. Good. Thank you.' Denys said at last, taking the money. 'We'll be right on it.'

'Should I sign something?' the man asked, raising a quizzical eyebrow.

'Oh, yes. Of course. I'll give you a receipt now and get my...um...secretary to draw up a contract for this afternoon.'

'Well, excellent. Thank you, Mister...?'

'Wilson, Denys Wilson.'

Thank you, Mr Wilson. We will be in touch. My employer is most keen that the...person in question...is tracked down a.s.a.p. I'm sure you can expedite the matter.'

'You can have every confidence Mister...' Denys glanced at the card. 'Mister Barrow.'

'I'll say goodbye and leave you to look over the file. Any questions, anything I can do to help, don't hesitate to ring me.'

'Thank you.'

The man left and Denys returned to the back room, grinning. Judith looked at him as he waved the cash at her.

'Wow!' said Judith. 'Result.'

Denys went to the window and raised a slat of the blind. On the pavement below he saw the man hurry out of the door. A black Cadillac stood parked outside, hazard lights flashing. Impassive by the car stood a woman: she was wearing an expensive little black dress and had a William Morris pattern silk scarf tied over her head. She looked middle eastern and appeared to be in her mid thirties. She held a small lapdog. The dog looked like a miniature whippet.

The man opened the back door of the car and held it open for the woman. Suddenly she looked up: big, deep, soulful eyes of amber and black stared up at the office window. Denys felt as if he had had an electric shock. He gave a low whistle.

'She's a bit of a babe!'

'Babe?' Judith said, 'She's a goddess.'

Sorcery had been a secret vice for Denys. He'd messed about with Golden Dawn style ritual magic but had quickly come to hate all the quasi-Masonic, hierarchical Victorian trappings and attendant bullshit. Chaos Magic had been his punk. Now he was just a low down hedge-wizard; basic sympathetic magic, hitting off networks of correspondences, a web of mutual mimicry with no positive term. Sigils, talismans and amulets.

It turned out quite a few people shared his private interest. In the early nineties James Rankin had introduced him to the so-called Spectral Situationists, to more or less orthodox surrealists, tankie god-builders, sweet but ineffectual anarchists and mad bastard anarchists, reichians, chaos mages and a cell of Posadists, followers of Juan Posadas, trotskyite and ufo cultist. It was a loose alliance, shifting and impermanent. They called themselves the Invisible College and hatched plans to overthrow capitalism with magic.

High weirdness in squats and patches of land by canals; rites and ceremonies under railway bridges and in underpasses; old gods called in echoing, empty warehouses. Barbaric names ululated in woods and public parks after the gates were locked.

That was how Denys had first met Judith. The College had briefly adopted Rhodes' idea of the Proletarian Satanic Mass. The medieval Satanists, Rhodes claimed, worshipped the 'god of the serfs' and were part of the class struggle against nobles and church.

They'd broken in to a deserted Church near the Finchley Road. The congregation sat in the mildewed pews swigging cider and Special Brew. In the vestry Denys and Judith prepared: a slice of turnip dyed black for the host; water in a pewter chalice, had from a charity shop. They had me briefly a few times before and liked each other. Judith peeped shyly from beneath a fringe of purple hair, shivering in an outsize pink mohair jumper. Denys was in all over black with spiked black hair. They nervously ran over their lines. There was a palpable sense of magical tension in the air. Judith was to be the naked living altar; Denys would fuck her as part of the ceremony.

'I'm fuckin' nervous.' Judith had said. 'I won't have to take it up the arse or anything will I?'

'No babe, not on a first Black Mass .'

Denys had given her a sweet little peck on the cheek and squeezed her hand.

'Ok, let's do it.'

Denys had met a lot of them then. Xaos Dave, Bloody Mary, Priesty John.

Denys remembered seeing Priesty John for the first time, standing in the middle of a Stop the City riot in his outsize greatcoat and holding a gnarled staff. He was surrounded by police with batons raised, their dogs straining at the leash, snarling as Priesty John raged, spittle flecking his sallow, unshaven face.

'I call you down Urizen, call you down from your high place…weeping in Golgonooza…Los and Luvah…we pour out…love and righteous wrath…rise up, Albion…rise up…'

He was still doing the Behmenite and Blakean thing.

'Would that all the Lord's People were prophets.'

The police batons never fell on him, the dogs never bit.

Fiery angels stood about him and kept him safe.

Xaos Dave had said: 'Never met a god I really liked.'

'Work with - not worship.' Bloody Mary had added.

The Invisible College had produced a few issues of a paper like *Class War.* Four page cut'n'paste: *Hexed* it was called.

The Charles and Diana cover had caused some bother.

Headline: 'Consider yourself fucking CURSED!' above a picture of the couple as dolls pierced by pins. Questions had been asked in Parliament. 'My god, these proles are using nothing other than BLACK MAGIC...' spluttered an apoplectic Tory from the shires, cowshit on his boots...and only a few years later.

Then the inevitable splits, magical battles, sitting in bedsits getting the fear.

The basic problem is that Capital is neither here nor there, it is all or nothing, 0 or 1, an amorphous and all-pervasive magical egregore, call it Mammon or Urizen, that paradoxically deploys a profoundly anti-magical semiotic war machine that consumes real bodies, real matter. Individual companies and corporations have powerful hoodoo on their side to be sure - logo sigils, copywriter's barbaric names, thought-form bullyboys - they also have lawyers. And the police and ok, so you pick off one member of the board, take out a whole board...

MISSING CORPORATE EXECS FOUND; 'We were on a team building exercise, paintballing, then suddenly there were all these weird lights in the woods - PANIC - it was like Lord of the Flies - only two of us staggered out, bloodied and limping... we knew we'd been hexed...'

…and what then? Another bunch of bastards just the same. Or send in a servitor to fuck up the accounts, IT, whatever - they go under and another two spring up to replace them. This side of the barricades it's finding the symbolic sweet spot, setting in motion the cascade of circumstance - butterfly effect - cat's whisker - we are trying to get through…

Denys paced about the office. Judith had left her laptop open on the desk: a horoscope on the screen. Denys gazed at it. He didn't know much about astrology but he let it speak to him:

Venus and Jupiter are inharmoniously placed: the Patient will be idle, given over to voluptuary practices and futile rebellion.

Pisces is afflicted suggesting impostumations in the Stomach.

The signs are marked on the ecliptic of the M25. Aries ingresses at Rickmansworth. The midheaven is at South Mimms service station.

Mars is conjunct Saturn in Virgo and the 2nd House: this notes eczematic gout.

Mercury is badly placed at the Angel in St. Giles designating Vertigos, Phthisis, dry coughs and all evils in the Fancy.

Malefic aspects crowd Gemini, London's sign. Uranus is in the tenth house in difficult aspect to the Sun which stands on the Imum Coeli. Expect tumults, the overthrow of governments, revolutions and the death of leaders.

The Red Lion at Richmond is in Taurus: beware the King's Evil, Wens, Fluxes of Rhuems falling Into the Throat and Quinzies.

The Fixed Star Prima Hyadum, the northern eye of the Bull, exerts its baleful rays. Wise Ptolemy gives tears, fierceness, weapons and fevers, and contradictions of fortune under this star. If culminating it results in disgrace, ruin and death.

Question: Is Prima Hyadum culminating?

Answer: It is.

Neptune in the 5th is indicative of incipient alcoholism; the pile-up in Aquarius means melancholy winds coagulated in the Veins.

Beware a fair-haired man with a goitre and a limp. He is holding a pair of scissors.

Give it all up.

The pale rose star Aldebaran stands over Alexandra Palace - this star *can* give honour, intelligence and courage: in *this* case a serious attack of the squits is more probably indicated.

The harmonics are well and truly fucked, the midpoints are worse.

Pluto is retrograde from Brixton to Norwood - it doesn't bear thinking about.

A Primary Progression would tell us of the Patient's future but to what point?

For the 8th House is the house of Death.

Give it all up.

The 8th House represents the Estate of Man deceased; Death, its quality and nature. It signifies fear and anguish of mind. It rules the privy parts; it's colours, the Green and Black. The Hemorrhoids, the Stone, Strangury, Poisons, and Bladder are ruled by this House.

This is your lot. Give it all up.

The Moon is over the Lebanon Circle in Highgate; the Head and Tail of the Dragon mark Poplar and Ealing.

The Part of Fortune is at Charing Cross.

Judith came in from the back room. She sauntered up behind Denys and peered at the screen over his shoulder.

'Not good. Bloody terrible, in fact.' she said as if stating the obvious.

'Yeah?' Denys grunted. 'Nothing…nothing going for it?'

'Well, if you're into Lunar Mansions, that's the…um…the Crown of the Forehead…that's ok…yeah, from the Arabic… means Crown of the Forehead.' Judith replied, tapping her temple.

'Oh right. What's that mean when it's at home?'

It signifies amelioration of misfortune and the strengthening of love.'

'Well…that's not bad. Could be worse. Some hope there I guess.'

'S'pose so.' Judith said absently as she wandered off.

'Personally, I think Lunar Mansions mean jack-shit.'

LONDON P K HOT

Proletarian Black Mass.

In the room next door someone is clattering around. Muted white noise hiss and then voices. 'The television is ghosting.' a woman's voice says. 'It won't work right, Frank.'

The cats-whisker tickles the crystal. Nothing…then a whisper through the static. Interrogation of a dead man by a man living on borrowed time.

…need to get a Lethbridge fix on this place.

A suburban living room. A book open, tossed upon a chair. The book is called *A New Science of Navigation*.

I am on a train reading a book. It is called *A New Science of Navigation*.

The film now showing is called *Never Eat Seaweed: A New Science of Navigation*.

The compass rose; the needle spins then settles.

Freshening winds, blue skies…

'Anyone can make a cup of tea.'

Proletarian black mass.

'Not at all…they are…' The Minister shrugged and closed his eyes, as if at a loss to convey the depths of his contempt for the faction.

'The Invisible College', he continued, 'is based on a secret sodality of Black Magi who were involved from the very beginning in the formation of the communist movement. So-called dialectical materialism is the exoteric form of their philosophy. The esoteric doctrine of this inner cabal is known to very few.'

Haining froze; he could not conceal the horror that went to the very core of his being.

LONDON P K HOT

Esoteric Black Fallen Crow faction - outshone - Time muted closer - rain - the eyes then - fix static - splodgy papers esoteric burned - says he parapets glides - make beyond the rebrand - buried trailing - beneath is most - unwilling chill prison poets - knowledge to bird fired Magi - they four-dimensional glides - ready other offices door - before as esoteric nether form - looming Invisible Aeons falling - that pass the telling colours - now in nothing from falcons winds - my tarmac foggy - there Interrogation lies - way embers rant - the things LONDON and cabal that have white - mathematically room - light groping grown dead fog - and all Navigation - the rain whisper flecks the Underground - a loss is reverent - his apprehension a fog - freshening given these dead - and the Court make restrictions - reporting Science mass - not stations film a fog - with Court called other - LONDON P K HOT

Chris the Greeks' café was more properly a caff. Red and white checked oilcloth on the tables; red, brown and yellow plastic bottles, sachets of salt and pepper in a white bowl. Sugar in shakers. Steam and the smell of bacon. Breakfasts all day and kleftico that fell off the bone from noon. Chips with everything. Redtops only on a wooden table by the counter.

The builders were in in force; muddy work boots, fluorescent safety jackets and yellow helmets.

'Oi you dipstick where's me bread and butter?'

They were working at a building on the next corner down; for as long as Denys could remember the shop front had been boarded up.

Chris clocked Denys and raised his eyebrows.

'Yep...the usual.' Denys answered the unspoken question.

The only spare seat in the place was at the table nearest the counter. Alone sat Two Bags John with a cup of tea and a flapjack. Two Bags was normally in earlier for breakfast (tea in a cup not a mug, toast not a fry-up) and Denys wondered what he was doing here in the middle of the morning. He made his way towards Two Bags' table.

Who *was* Two Bags John?

That he was called John and always carried two bags was a given. Two Bags John always wore a dark gray suit, white shirt, sober tie and a trilby. The hat was not worn at a rakish angle but sat four-square on his balding head. Slim and in his early sixties. Polite, punctilious and prim; slightly prissy in fact. A tight, forced smile: you could almost hear the lip muscles creak. Lived with his mother. It was presumed he had a job of some sort but no one was clear what he did.

One bag was a brown battered leather briefcase, the other a large, squarish black case of the type favoured by travelling sales representatives. No one had ever seen inside them. They sat at his feet in the café and, if anything needed to be removed, John placed the bag on the table and tipped it towards himself, opening it just enough to allow the required item to be carefully abstracted. Sadly, nothing more exciting than a tiny notebook had ever appeared. Two Bags John would write in it with an equally tiny silver propelling pencil. Scrupulous, minute handwriting.

Speculation abounded as to the contents of the bags and the consensus of the café regulars was that they contained a Jack the Ripper-ish assortment of knives and surgical instruments with which he set about the gruesome business of horrible murder. Always the quiet ones and he did have the air of a whispery-voiced woman-hating Anglican.

'Do you mind if I join you, John?' Denys asked Two Bags.

The tight smile: 'Be my guest.'

'How's it going?'

'Well...um...everything is...um...satisfactory.'

'Busy.' Denys said, looking around at the workmen.

'Yes. In fact the present building work is the reason for my presence here at this untimely hour.'

'Oh, right. Why's that?' Denys enquired.

'Yesterday the foreman, in a casual exchange in this very establishment, mentioned that they have been opening up the old building at the corner. It was once a chemist's shop. He also mentioned that there was some sort of old radio set in the office adjacent to what was once the shop floor. Now, I happen to have a keen interest in vintage radio and rather invited myself along to see the apparatus in question.'

Denys was astounded. Two Bags had never been so loquacious: his usual idea of sparkling conversation was to contribute an attentive silence to any discussion, offering only the tersest reply if a direct question made silence impossible.

Today he seemed to be in the mood to abandon this minimal approach and talk. Denys was excited but resolved not to show it - wait, wait and then, casually; 'What's in the bags, John?'

'Oh, right. Vintage radios.'

'Especially crystal sets. That is my main passion.'

'I'm not sure...what is a crystal set?.' Denys asked.

'What are Crystal Sets? I am glad you asked! It is a fascinating subject. It dates back to 1920 when Marconi first started experimenting with radio broadcasting from his station 2MT in Chelmsford...'

Denys immediately lost focus.

'...earliest listeners to Marconi's radio programmes... used the most basic of radio sets called a Crystal Set...built one yourself, perhaps only a few shillings...didn't require electricity or expensive batteries...rely entirely on the electrical energy developed between the aerial and earth connection... tinkerers and experimenters...produce sounds as if by magic.'

Two Bags paused. 'Are you following this?' he asked solicitously.

'Yeah. Absolutely. Fascinating. Do go on.' Denys made an effort to follow this time.

'The crystal set had to be carefully tuned into the station by making adjustments to a tuning coil and condensor and by using a 'Cats Whisker' - lovely phrase - as the detector...the Cats Whisker was a fine wire that rested on a piece of crystal, usually galena, and had to be very finely adjusted to obtain the loudest and clearest sound. Once the 'sweet spot' was found it was important not to move it. It wasn't always galena; they used lumps of coal in the makeshift radios they built in prison camps in World War Two...Colditz and all that.'

There was a brief clatter as Chris set down a bacon sandwich and mug of tea for Denys.

Two Bags John continued: he had unlocked his word-hoard at long last.

'I will never forget the wonder when I first saw and heard a primitive radio working. It was 1951 or '52 I think. I was eight or nine and my parents had taken me round to my grandparent's house for Sunday dinner. They lived in a small house full of Toby jugs and wax fruit.

Anyhow, on this particular day, we were clearing the table and my Grandad turned to me and said, "John, how about I show you how to make a radio. How me and the lads did it, when I was in the army. Out of practically nothing!"

We spent the rest of the afternoon putting together the set. Grandad had a roll of insulated copper wire and we ran it the length of the garden as an aerial. Another length of wire was fixed to a metal spike and driven into the ground as an earth. Yet more of the wire was stripped and used to make a coil by winding it round a short piece of dowel. The whole lot was connected to some headphones and then Grandad produced a razor blade with a flourish.

"Careful, lad." he said to me, 'This is VERY sharp.'"
John laughed softly, fondly: remembering.

'What was the razor for?' Denys asked him. He was fascinated now.

"It was the crystal detector! The razor blade was added to the circuit and, headphones on, Grandad slowly played the loose end of the coil wire - the 'cat's whisker' - over the razor-blade.

"Got something." he said after a while.

He pulled the headphones off and handed them to me. I put them on and at first could hear nothing but static hiss. Grandad moved the cat's whisker a fraction and suddenly, faintly but distinctly, I could hear music.

It was *"Blue Tango"*, by Ray Martin and his band.

There I was, me and this amazing machine. I was hooked and I've been making the damn things ever since.'

John fell silent. Denys was moved. He could see the young John bent over the table, headphones on, his face radiant. His Grandad, his head slightly bowed was standing behind John, a loving hand on the boy's shoulder. It was dusk. There was a small lamp with a threadbare, fringed shade patterned with roses fighting a losing battle to keep back the gloom. Denys knew they were on a meter and that they wouldn't put the top light on until you could barely see.

Two figures in a bubble of light. Faintest whisper of music in a quiet, darkened house.

'Edward...Ted.' Denys said softly, involuntarily.

John started. 'Yes, Ted. That was my Grandfather's name.'

he said looking at Denys with surprise and suspicion.

Denys blew softly through pursed lips: 'Must be psychic.' he said and was relieved when the foreman bustled over to them.

'Sorry Gents. Bit of a hold-up. Just waiting on a skip. I'll give you a shout. 'Bout twenty minutes?'

As the foreman walked away chivvying the builders to get a move on as he went, Denys pre-empted more questions about his brief   by diving in with a question:

'So, are there many crystal set fans out there?'

'Oh, more than you would think. Brian Snelling was THE man, of course, but he came to a tragic end. Not that long ago in fact.'

'What happened?'

'Well, he was murdered. The police said it was horrible... never seen anything like it. They called it a ritual killing.'

Denys thought about John's bags and it's speculative contents and then checked himself, feeling the thought was an unworthy one. He indicated that John should continue with a slight nod of the head.

'In the world of crystal set radio everyone knew Brian Snelling. He was a tireless experimenter, a real purist. For Brian diodes and valves were works of the devil, where the rot set in with wireless. He was reputed to be unable to utter the word 'transistor'. His series of articles on high impedance headphones are classics.'

Denys nodded assent as if this was common knowledge.

'There's been a fair bit of crankiness in the world of wireless. Sir Oliver Lodge was an early pioneer - several inventions to his name - very clever man. He was also interested in psychic research. Testing mediums and all that. He hoped to communicate with the Spirit World via radio.'

Denys was on home territory now and listened closely.

'Marconi too: he claimed to have received messages which he attributed to...um...Martians.' John sniggered slightly.

'Brian sadly went down that route. He started dropping hints of some amazing breakthrough in letters to the *Crystal Set Bulletin* and various internet forums. Communication with other dimensions or worlds or somesuch. Very sad. The notes he sent out to fellow enthusiasts became more and more disjointed and unintelligible. *The Bulletin* stopped publishing his contributions and many people cut off contact. Just before he died he sent out a flurry of ramblings; final bulletins from a mind at the end of its tether: *"A New Science of Navigation"*. But even if we accept that Snelling was suffering from some form of mental illness it does not explain the final and horrible circumstances of his death...'

The foreman was suddenly beside them: 'We're opening up the front now if you want to come and have a look-see.'

John sprang to his feet and picked up his bags: 'Oh, excellent. Would you like to come Denys?'

'Yes, I'd love to.'

He wanted to know what had happened to Brian Snelling.

Outside on the street the foreman explained that the place had been sealed up maybe eighty years before. The daughter of the proprietor had inherited the building and had lived upstairs there all her life. Bit of an eccentric. Sometime before her father had died, they had simply shut the door on the shop and left it. Now she was dead and they were clearing the place.

'Upstairs is all faded chintz and the smell of cat's piss.' the foreman said.

'There's a door inside into what was the chemists shop: I punched through a panel and saw the back office with the radio thing that you're so interested in. I haven't been in properly as we had to prop up the ceiling by the door; it looked like the whole bloody lot was going to come down. We're going in through the old front door to the shop.'

The door had just been jemmied open and they stepped through. It was dark but as their eyes grew accustomed to the dark they could make out the bulk of the counter. There was a grind of metal and some good humoured swearing from outside as one of the sheets of corrugated iron was prised loose. A shaft of sunlight sprang across the shop. The three tun-bellied Rosamund jars still standing in the window sent kaleidoscopic splashes of red, green and blue across the pharmacy. Constellations of dust eddied in the air.

The place *had* been left perfectly intact and Denys stood, breathlessly taking in the dusty, faded glory: Kodak films, vulcanite, tooth-powder, sachets, and almond-cream;
a dispensary stove, cayenne-pepper jujubes and menthol lozenges, the glass-knobbed drawers that lined the walls - cardamoms, ground ginger, chloric-ether, and dilute alcohol, a graduated glass on the counter, the seductive shape on a gold-framed toilet-water advertisement. Blaudett's Cathedral pastille, ammoniated quinine, asthma-cigarettes, Christy's *New Commercial Plants* and the old Culpepper.

The daubs of red, blue and green light caught the knobs of the drug-drawers, the cut-glass scent flagons, and the bulbs of the sparklet bottles. They flushed the white-tiled floor in gorgeous patches; splashed along the nickel-silver counter-rails, and turned the polished mahogany counter-panels to the likeness of intricate grained marbles—slabs of porphyry and malachite.

The three of them stood silently for what seemed a long while and then the foreman gave a low whistle. There was sound of a sudden commotion from outside.

'I'd better see what it is.' said the foremen and returned to the street.

With the silence and their reverie broken John suddenly came to. He hurried through to the pharmacy office and Denys followed. It was dark but they could make out a writing desk and next it that a table heaped with frail coils of wires, old-fashioned batteries and rods in front of a brown Bakelite casing that sat against the wall. There was a dial and various knobs on the casing and some headphones were plugged into a jack.

John was moved, almost ecstatic. He rattled off the names of the various parts excitedly, too quickly for Denys to follow.

'... but the magic--the manifestations--the Hertzian waves-are all revealed by this. The coherer, we call it.'

He picked up a glass tube not much thicker than a thermometer, in which, almost touching, were two tiny silver plugs, and between them an infinitesimal pinch of metallic dust.

Denys reached for the large tuning knob and turned it.

'The batteries are long dead. Best not touch.' John said.

A faint light came on within the casing, glowing through the louvered top.

'Impossible!' John cried.

Over the radio from the dusty headphones. - *hiss of static* and then an erratic Morse backed by what sounded like a tinny kazoo fading in and out: it was the Music of the Spheres.

Denys heard a quiet voice over the ether; it pronounced one word: 'Isis.'

No more voices but the sound of an echoing, impossible tune rose and fell.

Two figures in a bubble of light. Faintest whisper of music in a quiet, darkened house.

GHOST PHARMACY OPENED

Cunning man calibrates Hieronymus reading accessories in spectral detection apparatus.

Ghost shrack! Smell of similar contraptions. Letter of introduction required. Down in the windows before the tun-bellied rosamond jars, behind the counter many electrics: it is one of our more novel innovations relating Corbusier-style pharmacy.

Crystal set, cat's whisker log.

The mad hindoo panties down. She's wet and ready; marble slabs supernatural. One may use our products to detect old Culpeper signals hertzian waves. Plate-glass the likeness of intricate grained satin bow tops.

Stains arcane knowledge...pneumatic east. Gothic pile but including stethoscope, elbow length occult requisites and sundries.

Mr T A Hornimann's catalogue got the knack of the unintelligible over the radio....static and then a gleaming leprosy on the sky.

Chill jars - red, green, and blue blazed in the broad London supplier of scientist who disentangles a hard-on from his corduroy porphyry and malachite.

Blaudett's big science gloves and debouch magnesium yellow light flecked with analyses.

Ghosting in on the modern.

Thrills a toilet-water advertisement.

Our electric lights, set low violet, feeble aurora; cup of tea steaming a traveller: Mr Hornimann, esq.

Concatenation of the drug-drawers, contains a plethora of devices designed using the latest ghosts.

Initial data:

First communication: we are counter-rails and turned the polished mahogany illusory now a raven-tressed enchantress... honey-potted the mad dead.

Conversation between a dead man and a man living on borrowed time.

Opaque white stockings with embroidered windows. There was a confused smell of trying to get through.

Manners here among the whispering dead; they wanted to be elsewhere and were just hanging around - almost absolute zero.

Denys never quite able to supply Lethbridge devices and called cut-glass scent flagons and the monstrous daubs of red, the music of the spheres.

Wireless better offer. He had white coat, wild hair and eyes, the works: reiteration blue and green, bulbs of the costume, space and time. Policy wonks of the astral plane; scientist.

Eyes wide brings her hands to her mouth. Once tubes, lights, tesla coils and van der graaf generators - this injurious to human well-being.

For the seasoned traveller revealed this: the coherer. We telegraph odyle!

Mad scientist vibe on manufactured screaming method.

Big spark 136-142 Holloway road, alcohol.

A graduated glass.

The discarnate beings, unnatural creatures vulgarly called monsters. Those electrical discharges in the air, vacuum red, now have him leashed and used for his eldritch spectral worm!

The seductive shape on a gold-framed crumple villa with world.

Alchemy of the word. Method!

'The stars, harrumph, the stars are tired topologies and typologies, mired in his sweat, fags and booze: suddenly he enters scientific principles to answer all your needs regarding the Lethbridge scale. Lit by the globes dealing out fiery gnosis...'

Half-lives and experimental lozenges. The glass-knobbed drawers counter-panels kaleidoscopic lights on the faceted knobs undertaken. Lined the walls - cardamoms, ground ginger, chloric-ether, catalogue available on request.

Bespoke commissions with modern people on board. Necessary stench as we improvised from a nurse's gin-soaked colonial in the far borrowed time.

Demand the bona fides of these; skimpy dress rides up exposing her stocking glass gods. Blossomed, an unaccountable and menthol blond assistant, sparklet bottles. They flushed the white-tiled we believe playing a praeterhuman intelligence. Her tits are spilling from the unbuttoned top - the generator crackle and spark, reek of ozone. Gorgeous patches splashed nickel-silver.

We are already elsewhere.

Rewrite with new back-story: the pneumatic blond, utmost discretion assured.

Gentlemen callers only may scream, A hunchback cackling pulls the lever. Plants and the move onto the glacial plateau, flickering crimson, almond-cream. Dispensary stove - cayenne-pepper jujubes tantrism.

Films, vulcanite, tooth-powder, sachets, dilute say? No more stories, never trousers and pulls her white linen suit. That electricity! magnetism!

Of her quickly and fucks frenziedly: he comes waiting for her again.

Surfing surface; glitter of light on water; Morse backed by a tinny kazoo fading in and decked out in orris.

Kodak tiled floor wearing a suit. Terminated if bothersome or possibly narrative. Niche marketing of story thread.

Endless cathedral pastille, an asthma-cigarette, Christy's new ghostly spin doctors: Circumlocution Office of the other.

A church hall near Norwood. Pensioner's and mothers with young children. Unemployed men. Quiet expectation and tea and biscuits. Tubular metal chairs with fraying canvas seats.

On the notice board outside:

SEE!

Dr. Dexter
and
his Prophetic Film Organ!

Wonders of the World!
Glories of the Past
and
Marvels of the Future!

Entry! Refreshments GRATIS.

Lights down: mother's hush their children and the crowd falls silent.

Sepia film flickers on the screen. Prophetic images of coming tumult. Figures rush along London streets in panic. A sense of impending doom over all. Fiery eldritch shapes over Peckham Rye. Alexander Palace lit with a pale blue haze of static, the radio tower broadcasting messages of black and gold nothingness. Parliament ablaze. Gog and Magog step down from their plinths in the Guildhall and rush into the streets of the City of London hurling besuited passers-by screaming into a vortex of digital spirits.

They are sucked dry - husks of bodies. Even the dead are not safe; ghosts dying a second death. Night time, city skyline: the stars go out.

Images end in blank brown-yellow, 5-4-3-2-1, blips jumping on screen. Then finished. Thwapp, thwapp, thwapp of the film reel in the dark silence.

Then pandemonium: terror sweeps the mute spectators who break into inarticulate cries and tears. They rush from the church hall in panic-fear and stand bewildered and sobbing in the churchyard..

Doctor Dexter aka the terrible Deadman stands stock still behind is antiquated film projector and smiles.

Denys bundled into the office: he carried a carrier bag.

'Been shopping?' Judith asked, looking up from her laptop.

'I want to get this Missing Person thing going.' he said.

'So you've been shopping then? Anything to eat? A morsel of chocolate? Maybe a bag of Cheesy Wotsits?'

Denys gave a noncommittal grunt. He was unusually animated and seemed preoccupied.

He went over to a short shelf that held their library. The books were mostly Judith's: ephemeredes, the two fat volumes of William Lilly, *Astrological Aspects, Mundane Astrology, Horary of the Dream* and so on for a good yard..

Denys had a few paperbacks. There had been a fire a few years back and Denys had lost most of his books: an occupational hazard of combining Candle Magic with heavy drinking. A few remained: Raphael's excellent *Fortune Telling with Cards*, Sepharial's idiosyncratic *Book of Charms and Talismans*, Buckland's frankly bizarre *Magic of Chant-o-Matics*, Shah's infamously shoddy and inaccurate *Secret Lore of Magic* and Simon's totally fake *Necronomicon*.

It could be worse; they were certainly enough to get by on. Denys missed most the books of the *Bibliothèque bleu*: the *Petit Albert, Dragon Rouge, Grand Grimoire and Grimoire of Pope Honorius*. These works were usually described as corrupt, notorious or frankly diabolical. A real whiff of brimstone, that real magical glamour. He flicked through a couple of books and then put them back.

'Fuck it, I'll do it free-form. Improvise.' He went into the back office.

'Do not disturb.' he said. The door closed.

Judith thought she had given Denys long enough: he had been in the back office for over two hours and after some sound of movement and *sotto voce* chanting everything had gone quiet. She went over to the door and knocked quietly. No reply. She knocked again, louder.

'You ok in there?'

Again no reply. Judith opened the door.

Denys was sitting cross-legged in the middle of the floor. He was naked apart from a shapeless checked hat on his head. His eyes were closed and he was stock still.

In front of him there was a pipe, a magnifying glass and a hardbound library book. There was also a square of parchment with 2,080 written on it in purple felt pen. A small piece of lodestone, a few cloves and leaves of cinquefoil.

Judith stepped towards Denys: not a flicker. She tipped her head sideways to read the spine of the book: *A Study in Scarlet*, Arthur Conan Doyle.

'What's with the hat?' Judith said.

A pause and then Denys' eyes opened.

'It's a deerstalker. I am Sherlock Holmes.'

Denys and Judith awoke. The invocation of Sherlock Holmes the day before had produced no concrete results yet other than a deep *ennui* and a desire to assuage it with cocaine, a 7% solution. Denys had resolved to spend the day tracking down his man: he had no real idea how he was going to go about it but he felt the mercurial genius of Holmes within him. Inspiration would surely strike.

He padded over to the windows and drew back the curtain a fraction.

'Blimey!' Denys said.

'What is it, hon?' Judith said, her voice husky with sleep.

Denys pulled back the curtain with a dramatic flourish:

'Fog!' he said. 'A real peasouper, Watson!'

'We create high performance digital environments.'

Palimpsest of equations.

Synthesis of proteins.

Niche Marketing. Added value...

Knotty root, claggy brown clay glazed with rain.

'Wotz in tha placcy bag? fuck, there's clothes in the plastic bag. Whole lot swimming in blood, like a supermarket joint in tight clear wrap, y'know.'

Added value high performance digital environments.

Optimised black steel cabinet.

17% 000101010001011101010101010101 re-route re-route.

'Anyway, I was cutting through Highgate down to the Archway Road. I'd trogged all the way from Cricklewood...Shootup Hill. I'd lost my Oyster card but got a bus a bit of the way but then I had to change. I was skint and decided to walk the rest...it was pissing down...anyway, it was getting on, cold, perishing cold and pissing rain and dark and then out of the velvet dark the giant bat things came on softly whispering wings: they warped time about them as they flew...'

Muscle flex, spasm, fleshy torsion.

Knotty root.

We are operating at level 5 - amber - 21%

We are operating on a higher frequency.

Everything is now digitised.

Please select an option: press one for...

Time to get out of here...

Rhumb line and compass rose.

Quantum cosmogram.

Complex sigil of the Underground.

Denys and Judith were huddled by the patio heater in the beer garden having a quick fag.

'Oh fuck, it's Fat Bob.'

Denys felt the sense of well being engendered by his first sips of lager evaporating. He grimaced and then, seeing he'd been spotted, raised his pint glass in salutation towards the lumbering figure across the beer garden. He gave a wan smile of welcome. Fat Bob grinned and made a beeline for them.

Fat Bob was forty something and huge; tall and broad, beer-gutted. He was squeezed into a shiny grey suit, neck strangulated by a shirt collar still tight even though it is unbuttoned. The shirt, inexplicably, was maroon.. He seemed to move in slow motion with that strange grace of the half-cut; like a ballet dancing hippo he shimmied through the throng of drinkers. He had a packet of pork scratchings in one hand and a tumbler of something that looked like cough mixture in the other.

'It's Fat Bob.' Denys repeated to Judith as if it explained something.

'Friend of yours?'

'Yes...sort of...more an acquaintance. I don't know. He's around.'

'Awright Den...long time.' Fat Bob said through a gobfull of pork scratchings.

He gave Judith a frank appraisal. 'Whose the bird...you gonna introduce us?'

'This is Judith. Judith...Bob. Bob....Judith.'

Judith raised her glass: 'Nice to meet you.'

'How's it hanging? Still doing all that weird shit?' Bob

asked Denys.

'Yeah, still doing the weird shit. How are you?'

'S'allright...yeah, great.' Bob replied.

There was an awkward pause.

'Anyway, are you two...partners...or whatever?' Fat Bob asked bluntly, looking around as if hoping to spot a better conversational deal elsewhere..

Denys replied with flustered 'ums' and 'ahhs'.

'Yes.' said Judith, looking Bob in the eye.

'Ah, bollocks!' Bob said, looking theatrically crestfallen.

'All the good looking babes are always taken.'

Judith inclined her head in gracious acceptance of the compliment.

Denys opened his mouth to start a sentence but Bob beat him to it.

'Got a looker there, Den.' he said, 'Come for the tits....stay for the arse...awww!'

Denys normally chose his demeanour from a narrow range extending from mild confusion to frank perplexity, leavened by occasional blank incomprehension but now he felt that a different response was called for. He set his shoulders and tried to look both determined and chivalrous. Neither Bob or Judith seemed to notice.

'Oi...Bob, behave.' Denys spluttered.

'Jus' being friendly.' Bob beamed.

He downed the concoction in his glass in one.

'I'll get 'em in. I'll show you how to make a Raging Bastard.' Bob said. 'Let's make a night of it!' he added over his shoulder as he turned and headed for the bar.

Denys' heart sank.

'Seems like a nice bloke,' said Judith, 'Bit pissed though.'

'It could be handy, him turning up here...' Denys said, suddenly thoughtful.

'Well, he looks like he's up for it if you fancy getting hammered tonight. I'll probably bail out and have an early night if you don't mind.'

'No, the case...Bob could help...'

Before Denys could explain Fat Bob was back holding three tumblers of the cough mixture. Bob set down the glasses on a table and explained that the Raging Bastard was based on a cocktail called a Hot Mexican Hooker. It was his own invention. The original base was tequila, tabasco sauce and the juice from a can of tuna: Bob had augmented this with a shot of Red Bull and a secret ingredient which had still to be added.

Fat Bob fished through his jacket pockets, a detritus of betting shop pencils and wads of wonga and finally found what he was looking for.

'Aha!' he exclaimed holding up a small wrap of cigarette rolling paper.

The ends were twisted and there was a bulge in the centre: it looked like a little Christmas cracker. Bob deftly tore off one end of the packet and looked around with exaggerated caution to make sure no one was looking.

Everyone *was* looking.

Bob carried on anyway, he didn't give a shit, and sprinkled a fine white powder into one of the glasses. The powder was held briefly by the drink's meniscus before falling in slow constellations through the dark translucent liquid.

'And that,' announced Bob triumphantly, 'is a Raging Bastard.'

'What's that stuff in it?' Judith enquired.

'Speeeeed!' Bob said ecstatically. 'Good stuff too...none of that bathtub shit.'

Judith decided to pass on the Raging Bastard. She finished her lager and said her goodbyes. She left Denys looking rather green around the gills and starting to talk utter rubbish.

The rest of the evening was a blur. At some point Denys and Bob got a cab over to some awful dive in Ponders End; a drinking club full of roiling blue cigarette smoke and old guys playing cards. Formica tables and girlie calendars on the wall. Strip lighting too bright. Then on to a pub: too dark this time and edgy. Full of young men in cheap, paper-thin jeans and football shirts standing silently holding an orange juice or a half of lager. Probably all pumped on steroids. Denys and Fat Bob talking, talking, talking. Then out into the chill night air: Bob was swaggering but Denys had to concentrate on staying upright. He had one eye half closed for focus: the whole world threatened to go into a tailspin at any moment.

Bob seemed to know where he was going and Denys followed. Rows of terraced houses in deserted streets. A main road still busy: vague shouts and blur of car lights. Youths milling outside a chippie; sharp sting of the smell of vinegar. Quiet streets again.

They cut through a retail park with its hanger like buildings looming. Empty car parks. That went on and on.

Suddenly Fat Bob jinked between a large hoarding and

a wire fence and seemed to disappear. Denys stood swaying and confused. Bob's head popped round the hoarding: 'Oi, this way.'

Denys followed. There was a gap in the fencing behind the sign that led into a strip of overgrown land that ran between the fence and an outer perimeter wall. Bob hurried through the tall grass and nettles until they came to a patch where the wire fence was replaced by walling. They seemed hemmed in. Bob stopped and Denys almost stumbled into him.

'Right Den, lets get this sorted.' Bob said.

Denys wasn't sure at first what Bob was talking about but then realised dimly that his earlier drunken ramblings about the missing person case was about to bear fruit.

'Ok Bob - do you thing.' Denys slurred. He sat down involuntarily. Wet grass soaked the arse of his trousers.

Bob stuck out his chin. His teeth were grinding and he was flushed and sweating. He pulled his jacket off and ripped off his tie. His shirt followed. He stood with his legs apart and began to roll his head. His breathing began to come low and fast. Bob raised his arms slightly and clenched his fists. He closed his eyes briefly and then opened them again: his eyes were wide and unseeing, almost luminous in the dark.

Bob began to utter a series of low, bloodcurdling moans and to twitch uncontrollably. Suddenly Bob let loose a torrent of glossolalia: speaking in tongues. It made no sense at first but suddenly there was some clarity:

'…Thames - Thames - meet - Pim - Pim - Book and - Eff - Eff - Effa - part - parted…'

Bob lapsed into incomprehensibility again. Denys fixed

the words he had heard in his mind, repeating them over and over.

At last Bob stopped. His mouth worked silently for a few seconds and then he pitched forward face first into the mud. He lays still for a few seconds and Denys made his way over to the prone figure. Denys felt quite sober now as he helped Bob to his feet.

Bob blinked blearily and drew himself up to his full height. He breathed in and out slowly and deeply for a minute or so and then shook himself.

'Lost it there. Did I do the business or what?'

'Yes. Yes. Thank you.' Denys said quietly.

Gas looming minutest fragments through the fog - uprose goddess radiant in the streets - undimmed her way from spongey Green Park - travelling by these crabbed marks on crumpled paper - shops lit two hours before - Underground stations warm glow - the reverent and true unwilling look - raw afternoon - scraps of badly printed paper - the dense fog is telling fearful tales - muddy streets beyond the threshold - things about us in the world - to corporation Temple Bar - hard by Temple Bar Lincoln's Inn Hall - Chancellor in his High Court of printed papers - tawdry papers with no apprehension of the four-dimensional - being curious beyond - fog too thick - mud and mire in splodgy ink - hurrying on before with groping hand - dull fibrous texture - not what lies beyond - what is natural for us in this High Court of Chancery - foggy glory round his head - we should not need to think of cloth and curtains - communion and delight - punctiliously correct - hidden and disappeared cosmogonies of Chancery offices - kindling light life forms of the ether - weather-bow of my knowledge - fog in matter - instinctive universe - fog in the parapets of a nether sky - eddying back through seed - with fog all around them - treated mathematically sent back to prison - the empty court burnt away - a great planar space - let us speak of what seems strange there - beneath the spreading wind a sepulchral master stood - we suppose that we live in people says the Chancellor - dexterously vanished small particles of matter -prisoner is presented nothing charges of papers and carried off - what hangs before our faces - gazes see four dimensions - attend to it grown so cramped - follow the ready algebraist - came to the most distant lands - changed almost into what he sold - accessible through branded gateway in the unseasonable snow.

Denys made his way up the steps of the white concrete and glass building. It was a box-like moderne villa. The little card next to the buzzer to the top flat read JAMES RANKIN. Denys rang.

Brief electrical crackle and then: 'Who is it?'

'James, it's Denys.'

'Cool beans. Come on up.'

The door made a series of rapid clicks and Denys went in and up the stairs to the third floor.

James was standing at the open front door to his flat, smiling. He was slightly older than Denys but looked younger. Hair in a foppish flick; jeans and a checked shirt.

'Come in, come in. How are you?'

'Yeah, not bad. Some odd stuff going on I want to run by you.'

'Yep, no worries; I'll get a coffee on…or would you like something a bit stronger'

It was just eleven.

'I'll have a lager if you've got one. Mind if I smoke?'

'Balcony then.' James said.

Denys walked down the hallway. The bedroom door was open and a woman was folding up what appeared to be a white rubber nurse's uniform. She was beautiful: jet black hair in a severe bun, a pale almost white face, a black pencil skirt and a white blouse. She was a photo in frosty monochrome except for her vivid scarlet lipstick. Denys gave her a friendly nod but she ignored him, positively radiating indifference.

'Typical.' Denys thought. 'James always gets best shags. A casual charm and a keen mind. Its distinctly unfair.'

Denys made his way through the living room to the balcony. The big room was white walled with low black leather couches and armchairs.

Canvases of Pop art gods and Neo-geo sigils in luminous lime, lemon and orange were displayed on the walls. On a shelf were a number of folded paper figures: most were abstract geometric shapes but one complex piece looked like a horned demon. James had had a soto Zen period and experimented with spell casting by origami folding.

There was three old valve and tube televisions stacked one on top of the other against the far wall; they all looked like fifties and sixties models. Next to the televisions was a heap of scientific apparatus: a metal box with a large dial and an array of knobs, a Jacob's Ladder, Van der Graff generator, coils of copper wire. It was all part of James's Big Science thing: he'd always been into the psi and pseudo-science side of Chaos Magic. He claimed to be working on a mysterious manuscript called *A New Science of Navigation* that would explain his theories of Animist Marxism and hypercosmic communism.

The french window were already open and a light breeze wafted pleasantly in. Denys sat at the wrought iron table, stained rust red and orange by the rain.

James joined Denys halfway through his cigarette, putting a frosted bottle of Pils on the table. James had a coffee.

Denys outlined his problem with the missing man. He had only taken the most cursory glance at the folder that had been left with him and was rather vague.

'Youngish guy…middle eastern, Egyptian maybe…

Osman?…I forget the name. His sister is looking for him. Or his wife. Not sure which. I bumped into Fat Bob; he came up with something…cryptic.'

'Fat Bob? Did he do his shaman thing?' James asked.

'Yeah, still frightening after all these years.'

'What's he doing now?'

'Nothing. The same.'

'What did he say?'

Denys repeated as best he could what Fat Bob had pulled out of the ether: '…Thames - Thames - meet - Pim - Pim - Book and - Eff - Eff - Effa - part - parted…'

James wrinkled his brow in concentration. He went inside and came back with a small netbook and booted it up. He started googleing.

It only took a few minutes as James tried out various possible spellings of the words Denys had heard.

'Bingo.' said James. 'Thames is nice and easy. It's Pymmes Brook not Book. And it's Effra. They're all rivers of London.'

James went indoors again and reappeared with a fold-out map of London and a small box. James opened out the box and took out a silvered steel spiral pendulum.

'Map dowsing…we should be able to pinpoint where your man is.' James explained.

James relaxed and moved the pendulum over the map. Suddenly the pendulum started to swing in a small circle. James marked the area of the map beneath the pendulum with a cross in pencil. James carried on sweeping the map: several times more it started to describe tight precise circles and James marked the map again.

At last James was satisfied he had covered the whole territory.

'Well, looks like your man is spending a lot of time in different locations…or he's gone to pieces.' James said. He returned to his netbook and checked out the locations.

The marks on the map were all near the meeting place of rivers and their tributaries. Where the Fleet met the Thames beneath Blackfriars Bridge; where Pymmes Brook met the Lea at Ferry Lane in Tottenham; where the Graveney fed into the Wandle in Summerstown. Beneath Vauxhall Bridge the Effra flowed into the Thames and in Ladbroke Grove streams fed Counter's Creek.

'Can I borrow the map?' Denys asked.

'Yeah, no problem. It may be some use, hopefully.'

'Judith has done some horoscopes. You use a combination of natal and event charts in forensic astrology. She said that 'disappearance' charts are almost always death charts. Reckons the he's still in London anyway.'

'Everyone's always in London.' James said.

There was a click, click, click of high heels on wooden tiles. The woman appeared at the French windows. She looked meaningfully at James, arching a pencilled eyebrow.

James smiled. 'Time to go, I'm afraid. We need to meet soon; Priesty John is off on one and wants to talk. Tomorrow?'

'Right, yes. Tomorrow.'

He folded up the map and left.

Denys took a bus down Lordship Lane, then got off ambling up the Tottenham High Road. Half a mile or so heading towards White Hart Lane then turn left. A private road, entry barred by concrete bollards. A board :

Joint University Annexe

No Entry

These buildings are alarmed and patrolled.

To the left was a crumbling high wall, to the right a small glass and concrete building. Standard public architecture. Double doors chained shut. Empty library shelves seen through tinted glass. Dust breeding.

Past this building and turn a corner to the right: a portakabin and a flat-roofed single storey building of cement blocks and thin rusting metal window frames with peeling green paint.

Another notice was pinned to the portakabin door, printed on A4 and wrapped in plastic. The ink had smudged blue-black:

Anomalous Experience Unit (AEU)

Please knock.

The AEU was a specialist Psychology Department researching parapsychology. If it wasn't for a handsome bequest the Universities that jointly supported the Unit would have closed it down long ago. The Unit is widely considered to have 'gone native' and to be employing 'unsound methods'.

Denys headed towards the portakabin. The door opened

86

as he was about to knock.

'Hello, Denys.' Husky voice.

The owner of the voice stepped into the small yard. It was Professor Catherine Peyton: tumbled mess of black hair streaked with silver, white collarless man's shirt unbuttoned just enough to reveal a magnificent cleavage, the shirt untucked and flapping over long khaki shorts. High gray walking socks, honey yellow Caterpillars. Well-tanned and in her mid-fifties; also formidably clever. Originally an anthropologist she had turned to parapsychology and carved out her own little empire. Like Kurtz.

'Hiya. How's it going?'

'Good. You ready to get wired up.'

Denys visited the Unit once a week so they could run tests. It was fifty quid, cash in hand, for a couple of hours work.

'Quick rollie first.' Catherine said. She rolled a cigarette with practised ease. Denys declined a roll-up and had one of his straights.

'When we've finished this round of tests I'd really like you to do some real magic for us. We can monitor what goes on psychologically and somatically when you do your stuff.'

'I can't imagine that watching me light some candles or charge a talisman would tell you much.' Denys replied.

'I know, I know, but there are other forms that rely more on altered states of consciousness. Gnosis and all that. How do you charge a sigil, for example?'

She knew and Denys knew she knew.

'Generally, I wank off…or get someone else to do the job.'

Catherine licked her lips.

'Hmm…I promise not to look.' she said wryly. Catherine seemed to delight in unsettling him.

'There are other ways of doing it. Exhaustion…or …' Denys said.

'I'm sure there are.' Catherine said, cutting in. 'We'll get something sorted. Anyway, shall we…'

They made their way into the small building. The went into a small room. It was a white cube with a comfortable reclining chair in the middle. A large clock stood on a table against one wall. The clock had a Perspex casing and the cogs within could be seen turning with mechanical jerks: tick, tick, tick.

Catherine's assistants nodded a welcome. They were two young men, graduate students Denys guessed. He could never remember their names and had mentally dubbed them Thing One and Thing Two. They both wore expensive looking t-shirts in pastel colours and jeans that looked new. Well-muscled and tanned; hair sun-bleached. They busied themselves with some wires that lead from a black box beneath the chair.

Denys sat in the chair. Thing One placed a halved ping-pong ball over each eye. The idea was to create a mild sensory deprivation called the Ganzfeld. Thing Two threw some light switches: the strip lighting flickered off and was replaced by a low light with a soft rosy glow. Another switch lit a spotlight behind the clock and shadows leaped across the room: the inner workings of the clock were projected across the walls. The back of the chair was lowered and Denys was lying almost flat. Thing One stuck two sticky pads onto Denys's temples; they were connected by the wires to the black box.

'Something a bit different today, Denys.' the Professor explained. 'It's based on the work of Benson Herbert; he thought that clocks build up a 'mini-psychic environment' and you will try and influence the ticking of the clock. We will be recording the sound and videoing the mechanism's shadows to capture any disruption of its clockwork regularity. As usual, you are wired up to monitor your brain state.'

'Relax and concentrate on the clock ticking. When you feel ready try and alter the tempo of the ticking. We'll try it for fifteen minutes to begin with.'

Denys could see nothing but a warm pink glow. He heard Catherine and her assistants leave the room. The door slammed shut and then there was nothing but the ticking of the clock.

Denys tried his best but he didn't notice any alteration in the monotonous tempo of the clock. It seemed an eternity before he heard the door open again and hands removing the monitor pads and eye coverings.

Catherine suggested a break and they returned to the portakabin. One wall was entirely covered in shelves loaded with books, journals and box files. At the far end was Catherine's desk which groaned under notebooks, loose papers and computer printouts. Her computer screen had almost disappeared behind curling post-it notes. There were mugs and glasses and a bottle of whisky. Everything was lightly dusted with cigarette ash.

Catherine indicated a plastic chair for Denys to sit on. The chair stood in the middle of the room and Denys felt oddly isolated. It scraped it forward slightly.

Catherine sat on a grey swivel seat and opened up a mini-fridge beneath her desk. She fished out a tray of ice and fixed a large whisky.

'Want one?'

'Please.'

As they sipped the cheap spirit Catharine pulled up a graph on her screen. She pressed a button and a printer on the floor by her feet groaned into life; it laboriously ground out a metre long copy of the chart and tables of figures. Catherine looked over the printout and then swung round to face Denys.

'Not much. Bugger all in fact.' she said matter of factly.

Thing Two came in carrying an earthenware jug that steamed slightly.

'Oh, excellent…fancy some mushroom tea, Denys? It's pretty weak stuff and may help relax you for the next session.'

Denys knew it was a bad idea.

'Fine, I'll give it a go. It's pretty weak, right?'

'Just enough to give you a mild psychotropic lift.'

The Professor got two mugs and poured a little of the hot brownish liquid into each of them.

'You're having some?' Denys asked, surprised.

'I had some experience of hallucinogenic when I was an anthropologist. And recreationally as well of course.' Catherine said cheerfully.

Denys took a mug and cupped it in his hands.

'Down the hatch!' said Catherine. She downed her tea in one. Denys retched as he downed his measure.

'Let's give it half an hour or so.' Catherine said.

Denys felt uncomfortably hot and sweat prickled across his forehead. Catherine sat in with her legs extended in front of her. She was talking but Denys had lost the thread somewhere.

She was talking about the Batcheldor Method, whatever that was. Blips of coloured light flickered across Denys's field of vision. He became fixated on Catherine's breasts. The shadowy gap between them was deep and inviting and the texture of the flesh as they formed a deep valley seemed endlessly fascinating. Her tits suddenly seemed very close, looming up and threatening to engulf him. Denys felt as if he were sitting at right angles to his own body and then he was loose from his corporeal frame. His astral double shot forward like an arrow and into the comforting body heat canyon of Professor Catherine Peyton's cleavage.

Denys came round: there had been an indeterminate period of unconsciousness. He was standing in an alley.

Denys looked down the alley: it was very narrow - so narrow that if he met someone coming the other way he would have to squeeze past. He couldn't see the end of the alley as it doglegged sharply to the right about thirty metres or so down. It looked dank and grim.

Denys gave a shudder of apprehension but taking a deep breath he started to walk down the alley. He looked up: the walls rose up four or five storeys. Denys could see a small patch of sky above which looked gray and heavy with rain. The houses on either side seemed to lean inward as they rose up, giving a sense that the alley was closing up like a huge hand. Denys could see a few small windows that were yellowy brown with dirt - most were cracked. They looked down on Denys like blank, unseeing eyes.

Denys shivered and felt a sudden impulse to turn and run back to…wherever it was he had come from.

He felt a brief perplexity: he couldn't quite remember where he was or where he was going. He had a feeling he was near Charing Cross Road but it was only that, a feeling: he didn't recognise the alley and he couldn't get his bearings. Denys shook off a brief stab of fear then put his head down and walked on. There was a drip, drip, drip from the dank and slimy walls that looked rotten with age. The bricks and mortar were crumbling and bulged alarmingly in places. Large iron bars had been bolted to the wall to stop the brickwork sagging any further. Streaks of rust stained the wall beneath the ironwork.

Suddenly Denys heard a brief hollow laugh from above: a hollow humourless laugh. He looked up and saw a faint light such as a candle might make flickering through one of the windows above. There was a movement, a dark shape, as if someone had snatched a glance through the window and then retreated again into the shadows as if wishing not to be seen. The light was extinguished. Denys suddenly felt very cold and lonely: the shudder of fear ran through him again. He felt the urge to turn and run back but hesitantly carried on, his legs feeling like jelly.

Just before Denys reached the point where the alley turned he saw a peeling yellow poster on the wall. It had heavy black type that had smudged slightly. The poster looked odd: the lettering was a retro computer-style but the crude daguerreotypes looked Victorian. It said:

THE SINISTER DR. DEXTER'S TRAVELLING SHOW

Prophetic Magic Lantern Show!
Wonders of all Lands and Times!
Marvels to amaze young and old alike!
See: Ancient atavisms
AND
The latest Inventions of Modern Man!
The very Acme of Educational Entertainment!
Always showing!
In the **GUILD HALL**, Clerkenwell Road.

TO COMMENCE AT 8 O'CLOCK

Front Seats, 1 s. Back Seats, 6d.
Tickets to be had of Mr ROEBUCK,
Stationer at Clerkenwell;
and at the Guild Hall.

†††††††††††††

Denys looked closely at the engravings: they didn't do much to sell the show.

The central picture showed a man with wild white hair; he wore a frock coat and had his arms held aloft as if commanding the variety of odd contraptions about him. Denys presumed this must be the sinister Doctor Dexter - he looked like a mad stage magician.

Denys peered at the machines that surrounded Dexter: there were two spheres the size of footballs in a halo of sparks: a bolt of electricity crackled between them. The metal balls were wired up to Leyden jars and a large earthenware bottle that Denys guessed was a primitive battery. There were also retorts and other glassware that bubbled away.

Denys tore himself away from the poster. Sweat prickled across his forehead and he knew he had to remember something, something very important. More flickers of panic-fear. Denys found himself stumbling forward. He turned the corner of the alley and found that there were only a few tens of paces before it opened out into a street. Denys rushed forward and collapsed from the mouth of the alley into...

HIGH HOLBORN, 1745

A heat haze shimmered up from the dusty street and the few pedestrians dawdled along, keeping to the shadows. Windows everywhere have been flung open in hope of a cooling breath of air - there was none - and in the offices within it could be seen that even the most proper of gentlemen had doffed their wigs and loosened their collars. Flies were reduced to performing lacklustre, lethargic loops in the air and a lone dog, possibly mad, had given up and flopped down next to a water trough, an oasis in this city desert.

There was a distant clopping of hooves and, screwing up his eyes against the sun, Denys peered through the haze and saw a carriage appear. He knows where he is and when it is. Everything is as it should be.

The gilded phaeton made a stately progress down High Holborn. The horses sweated and strained forward as if the hot air had congealed and they had to push their way through it. They came to halt where Denys stood.

The driver of the horses was a portly man and seemed familiar to Denys. The Lady within was indistinct. She was obviously determined to see the sights of the great metropolis even if she melted in the task. With one hand she fanned herself as if she could dispel with a few magic passes the still, stifling heat. With her other hand she lifted to her nose from time to time a muslin bag containing a pot-pourri against the Great Stink that sat over London. It did as much to keep at bay the rank miasma as her fanning did the heat. A small dog was curled up in her lap. The Lady too seemed familiar to Denys: she had a look about her of Araby he thought.

The driver cursed the horses mildly and then looked at Denys.

'In this blazing midday sun one would not perhaps be surprised to see a line of camels picking their way from Charing Cross towards the City laden with orient silks and heady spices - who would otherwise brave this heat?'

'It is the very Sahara Desert!' the Lady exclaimed with effort from within the carriage.

It all seemed very wordy, very mannered, but Denys felt he should reply.

'Well, perhaps not the best day to see our glorious Capital: it is uncommon hot.' Denys said.

The Lady agreed that this was so.

'Nor indeed the best season. The place is turned to a veritable desert.' Denys continued.

The Lady did not demur.

'What brings you to London?' Denys asked.

'My family is here with my father.' the Lady replied. 'My father is pursuing his chymical studies.' she added, anticipating Denys's next question.

'Ah! A sooty empiric!' Denys exclaimed. ('What the fuck am I saying.')

'A sooty...empiric? What is that, Sir?'

'An empiric is one who labours by Experiment to woo secrets from Dame Nature. I say 'sooty' because the laboratory is fair hot and those who work there are often begrimed from the furnace.'

The Lady seemed amused at the thought of her father involved in unseemly manual labour.

'My father's work is most Philosophick - he is only begrimed by the scholar's lamp.' the Lady assured Denys. 'But we are all 'sooty empirics' in *this* heat.' she added with a tinkling laugh.

'Yes, indeed. And in a way we all are; we have all been given the gift of Reason, and as long as the light of Reason is not obscured by Enthusiasm or Skeptic Doubts we all may read the Book of Nature and come to know the Author of that

Book.'

The Lady looked puzzled.

'Authors...' she said vehemently.

Denys felt a sudden sense of unease. He had to remember something - to remember to remember...what...what was it? He looked about, suddenly distressed.

The driver and Lady seemed to lose focus; their lips moved but all Denys could hear was a confusion of noise, as if many people were speaking all at once. He looked up. From a doorway a gentleman approached: he carried two leather bags. The man removed his hat from his balding head and gave a tight smile. All Denys could see was the smile. It loomed up in a rush and seemed very close: he could feel the hot breath of the man on his face. Everything was blurred. The babble of voices turned to a strange hum, high pitched and non-human. *Static.* Hiss and blip. Denys was seized by vertigo. Everything suddenly went dark...

...chaos of lights and hiss of static. Denys came to. In front of him Catherine still sat on her chair. Thing One knelt at her feet painting her toenails. Thing Two stood beside Catherine massaging her neck: he was naked and had a hard on which the Professor was gently wanking.

'Back with us?' Catherine said abstractly. She had a beatific smile.

Without warning Denys was violently sick.

Contraptions about what lighthouse Clerkenwell Road - modern-ish for he was a team - attention immediately - and the peeling yellow poster nothing other than black so-called - looked like lettering accounts - sky above which left and walked on - he felt he had war seaweed in Leyden jars and a hubbled computer- to the bustle further streaks of hollow laugh from above - Denys out suddenly - hoodoo on their five storeys with Doctor Dexter - alarming radio arms held aloft as if bloodied - and beneath up at him again - huge heavy with rain the houses neither here nor windows above

7th flickering it read - even higher of the eyes - Denys commence at 8 o'clock - his very splutters and travelling show wall - back seats 6d. - most were on parliament mages - the basic feeling of fire breath - he started from the dank expositor of the sciences - sagging bolted to alley - he looked up: the magical king

He flipped the anti-magic war machine - hexed it was called bastard word movement - a dark then another could see a faint light - symbolic sweet spot by Doctor Dexter is wonderful - and a few something like these looked down the alley - wipe out years - magical egregore that senses walk down - the questions like Clerkenwell and coins - felt sudden impulse numbers - show wonders of all lands

Someone coming - the other brief prophetic magi - rust stained the letters on dark green - inevitable splits wall - odd back and claw - Denys could see all thoughts bubbled

- we'd been mused - cursed films he had seen - hangers-on smell of man - though linked up with a few book metres consuming the real - so again into the shadows of sparks - a street he's on and showing - whatever new science felt very cold god - these proles chemistry lab at school - large earthenware jar that Denys looked did read might - latest inventions rather - dressed didn't recognise pages at the machines - that amorphous capital of fear ran through him - little bodies small windows - that marvels to columns some engraved - spring up candle black type had said the sinister were spheres - produced picture of wired up acme of bricks - stop the brickwork with amazement

'Hmm!' they also have no language - hesitantly carried - asked them in to turn and run back about the same - the glance through got cowshit on his guessed barbaric names - and cat's whisker unlikely origami - the smudged slightly individual side looked gray - it was Doctor Dexter's - never words - slimy walls showed a wild haired sinister retreating - rose up giving woods panic - and Denys presumed to squeeze past - looked down the metal text on someone's yellowy edition

Much wall looked grim as if he voyages - opened the book at random and saw shock atavisms - problem remembering few - most were between primitive and moderne and commanding the Doctor Dexter - chaos up and sinister - the central picture you whole cabal - we sell the show - run limping - we knew they looked staggered out - his front the alley - which seemed to lean inward there - he had all or nothing 0 or 1 burned - around the image - looked for all the world like a navigation seemed rather old fashioned - put his nuclear physics & etc. - bolt books that cascade bedsits getting the fear thing

Black flies - shudder dropped the book - there was a drip, drip - Denys apprehension - replace light went rough and the name Doctor Dexter Dexter again - the ready shape of a crowned style - companies have surrounded the head white hexed - and so science museum make no sense but ironwork - now eat seaweed

Weighed yourself well and truly orthodox - sharply turned to primitive battery lantern - crumbling apoplectic seats - ancient shudder through the pages - the copywriter's Victorian rotted away long ago - it sure- logo sigils hypercosmic - mundane origami caught rotten with age - alley was closing up like them - weird lights in the suit servitor - a spectral electricity crackled the same unseeing cracked boots - renowned author of is Doctor Dexter esq. - dirt revised geometry carrier bag - something from police dimension

The paradoxically shivered earth was folding though in modern dress.

RISERS AND FALLERS	
UNITED UTILITIES GROUP	**618.50**
YOG SOTHOTH PLC ORD	**426.55**
BURBERRY GROUP PLC ORD	**1,546.00**
SMUG RICH BASTARDS 1	**584.50**
REED ELSEVIER PLC ORD	**544.25**
RANDGOLD RESOURCES LD	**5,570.00**
MAMMON HOLDINGS	**138.80**
FRESNILLO PLC ORD USD	**1,653.00**
VEDANTA RESOURCES PLC	**1,297.00**
URIZEN TECH	**455.70**

Refuse Urizen Tech bio apps.

Say no to Urizen Tech patenting your protein.

Don't listen to Dr. Dexter: his dismal science of protein synthesis and the 'realities of the marketplace' - extended phenotype of London - full tide of humanity at Charing Cross.

Leaf Insects and Dazzle Ships.

Stars and planets - extended phenotype of skeins of protein chains.

The radio is set to hissing static, garbled snatches of voices over the ether. The television runs a porn loop of a juicy fuck and cumshot, the usual. Ms C. L. O'Hara, porn starlet de jour moans as she takes it doggy-style from some big cocked hunk. Sigil on the television screen in wipeable marker pen. Judith is on the bed on all fours: curve of the back, gorgeous arse raised, long sexy legs, tits heaving in slo-mo time to Denys' thrusts; fucking into other dimensions. It's the zen porno tactic: desperate but it could just work.

A man is standing still and silent at the end of a baroque passage backlit by sunlight. He is dressed in black, very formal. Big Victorian beard. Behind him you can make out a formal Italianate garden.

'The dimensional rift is collapsing in upon itself!'

1st Communication: 'We are trying to get through.....'

Time televisions drift through warped space.

Mad scientists and sick sensitives.

'This case is exceptionally interesting. The shapes presented to witnesses did not seem to be objects so much as symbols.'

Thirties villa, white concrete and glass. Ghosting in on modernity. Gods made of electrons.

Diode and cat's whisker.

Voices heard on the threshold of waking, teetering on the edge of intelligibility. The dream state and the liminal state between sleep and awakening is a state of gnosis: fire off scattergun spells.

Car engine cut dead.

Vicar's wife breathless on phone.

Curious and burnished amber growth.

29 megacycles. The machine is operating. The crystals are magnetized.

Pinned by invisible fingers of sound.

Flames flickered all over.

'A dead person loses this hyper-dimensional thickness.'

Vanished in a cloud of unseasonable green snow.

A brass-cymbal led wilderness.

Fractal zodiac.

Swirls of unseasonable snow, moment of purest chill.

Masked hyperborean 'gods', burnished metallic costumes; barbaric and scientific. The world is scanned by the entities through their masks.

London Nuclear Alchemical Procedure

Letting your mind grow in murmurs - out your will - Azathoth
the other side - blood threatened to enter the fire - dispel with
veritable misfortune - run to the fire and let mustard emanate
from a nuclear plant - London lead falling to the floor - vomit
when air enters - pang of longing - it is hot razors - combined
women beating sun - one beginning - take bitch possibly mad
- holding back the biliousness - she thought overmuch on it
- resolved deep in its heart - given up on the relative street
- begin to avoid drinking water - you sooty empirics
- habituated to his plight - you are elementals performing -
and that pulsates

Visualize it she said - keep at stifling studies - it is uncommon
magic situation - I am merely glad that you hold off your teeth
- and bring familiar home - Charing Cross Road prepare to
perform the radiation - making the sickness grow - skeptic
doubts of electromagnetic radiation - through the next water
trough - know what she elemental should say - comb through
works - also rises out of your blood - 1745

A heat haze shimmers up - poisoning dismissal - blazing
midday power - remove thine conversation - I say alchemy
in the wires
Uranium 238 - a piece reduced to give the gift of reason -
and as pedestrians dawdle along - away from underneath
the high tension power lines - a piece of lead and something
vile that was raw - and manifest for five years - the effects

of radiation congealed - an empiric is one who labours - my family has fallen on hard power centre - absorbing from fire and black time - a muslin bag fire frock coat - several days before the elemental arrives - take the light of reason - in the steel provinces of your tight fist - and Punch mixed into Azathoth - High Holborn - ritual making over your head - shadows call the elemental towards the City - begin to chant iron - an electric blanket - high work over her demur - what windows everywhere - the laboratory is fair night - of high tension power - a sigil stranger - with one flicker spent all our elemental - and the anywhere oasis in the city desert

But now upon her a sigil of your season - London considered blackened - u238 silks and heady spices - fire heat bleeding on the night of the desert -the chymical lead high over you - emulate the elemental - making a stately progress down to you - by experiment to woo secrets with high tension power lines - brave this proper flesh - ship of polite fire - ladies have doffed their flesh - blue flame - throw it into the fire - the blue flame rises glowing.

They all met up in *The Orange Kipper,* a boozer in Hornsey. It had escaped being themed: a Victorian barn of a place with booths. Wisps of fog and cigarette smoke still lingered in the yellowed, ornately corniced corners.

Denys and Judith got there first; James Rankins was next, sans his frosty companion.

Bloody Mary walked in. She was an artist and had a 'space' in the Wood Green Cultural Quarter. She painted huge automatic canvases done Pollock style on the floor. Her blue boiler suit was speckled with paint; the black canvas of her skin was flecked with minute spots of red, green and blue. Quiet, almost demure in public, she was a mean sorcerer who performed ferocious sex magicks. Denys and Judith had once performed a ritual with her at her studio : 'Like being hit by a truck.' Denys had said. They had thrashed around naked in thick wet paint - abstract expressionist hypercosmic ideograms. Vortex leading to other dimensions. She was named Bloody Mary for her lunar gnosis: her decoctions of mystic syrops and rhums.

Xaos Dave sauntered in. He dressed smart: a dark gray suit and a leather case. He worked technomancy and liked the anonymous executive look: radionic apps and a virtual temple all carried on his laptop.

'How's Chas, Dave?'

'Still a bitch but he'll have to do until I get a better offer. What's the wig-wag?'

'We're waiting on Priesty...'

Dave got himself a drink and they talked shop for a bit. Bloody Mary and James discussed tangential tantra and

Duchamp's idea of the fourth dimension while Xaos Dave and Judith took up a long running argument about astrology. Dave had no time for astrology:

'…but the stars are alive!' Judith concluded.

'The stars, humph, the stars are a cold, pale leprosy on the sky.' Dave replied.

Denys smiled benignly and sipped his pint of lager.

'Where's Priesty then?' Mary asked after a while.

As if on cue Priesty John staggered through the pub doors. Greatcoat as usual, unshaven sunken face. He was clutching a crinkled Tesco carrier bag; the red and blue logo had worn almost away. Priesty John always looked on the verge of collapse and today was no exception. He looked wildly about and seeing his comrades sitting in a booth made his way unsteadily over, calling for a brandy and soda.

James went over to get the brandy and refills for the others. Priesty John settled himself and then pulled a grubby old map of London from his carrier bag. He made an ineffectual attempt to smooth it flat but gave it up. The map lay soaking up slopped beer from the table.

Everyone looked expectantly at the map: the ring of the M25 had been emphasised with green biro. Fragments of sorcerer's circles, a compass rose and horoscope wheels, all printed off from the internet, had been stuck along sections of the motorway. Priesty John's indecipherable scrawl made drunken spider curlicues across the chart.

'London.' Priesty began. 'The M25 describes a circle, like a magician's circle around London. But is it to keep something in or something out? This metropolis is the world: the original oecumenicus…'

Everyone listened intently. Denys welcomed a feeling of bafflement like an old friend.

'…the area between what is today New Oxford Street and Bloomsbury was once called the *Holy Land*. Rookeries of the low, warrens beyond the purview of so-called law and order. And the rivers of London…'

Denys and Judith sat up. Denys exchanged a meaningful glance with James who sat impassive, brow wrinkled.

'…the rivers of London are the rivers that run out of Paradise. Mystically, the Thames is the Nile, of course. The Fleet and so on, are the Tigris and Euphrates, the Ganges. Also the dark waters of the Cocytus, Acheron and Styx. Rivers of the underworld…subterranean…'

Priesty John was racked by a cough and faltered.

'Go on.' said Bloody Mary quietly.

'I have seen, I have seen…' Priesty John said.

They listened as Priesty John told them what he had seen. Denys truly saw it, saw it through Priesty's eyes.

****

"A sudden gust of wind bringing rain.

There was a moment of purest chill then the summer heat reasserted itself. Large drops of rain spattered the wide dusty streets. The smell of damp pavements…

I saw: **Asmodeus**, *who tempts with pride, now working as a gardener, clipping a privet hedge.*

I saw: **Dispater**, *who can find buried treasure and tell of what may come to pass flipping eggs and frying bacon in a greasy spoon.*

*I saw: **Balam**, who gives True answers of Things past present & to come, who maketh men to goe invisible, bored behind the counter of a newsagents, flogging Twixes and copies of the Daily Mail.*

They are Demons, once proud Princes of Hell taken human form. They are burned out. Their curse, the Fallen, is that they can create nothing new.

'Aeons of routine evil can take it's toll, mate, I can tell you.' Asmodeus told me, leaning over the hedge on a fag break. 'Trouble is, you bloody humans have got us beat all ends up in the evil stakes. Inventive, you lot, bloody inventive.'

Devils cannot make new evil but man can. The shame of being outshone by humankind has broken their spirit and they have left the Pit to come to London and its leafy suburbs...

New circles of despair...they live in crowded crumbling houses on the North Circular; the fumes and noise of constant traffic past the gardenless houses a pale reminder of the pandemonium of home.

Asmodeus, Dispater and Balam sit in the dank front room, chain smoking. Saggy second hand furniture, fly blown windows. Silver foil cartons hold the congealed remnants of last night's curry and cigarette butts amid a sea of empty beer cans on the low coffee table. Television on, loud against the traffic, screen flaring with overbright colour.

***Marchosias** bustles through the door carrying a blue carrier bag full of groceries. He is a great and mighty Marquiz, a strong fighter of the order of dominations. He governeth 30 Legions of spirits. He Told his chiefe Master who was Salomon, that after 1200 yeares he hadd hopes to returne* to ye 7th Throne in Heaven: some bloody hope. He is weary from a long, hard day working in the car park at Ikea.

'Bollocks, bollocks, bollocks.' he growls, nodding to the others as he crosses the room for the kitchen. Without looking away from the television they nod and grunt in acknowledgment. 'Today was bollocks. Really shit...anyone for a beer.'

Three more grunts, more enthusiastic this time, give assent.

Marchosias enters the small, grimy kitchen and with a shrug of his shoulders throws off his human form: he looks like a werewolf with a griffin's wings and a serpent's tail. He belches and a gout of fire flares from his mouth.
Padding across the sticky lino he opens the fridge and with massive hairy paws takes out a lager. He tries to open the can but his claw is too big and clumsy to lift the ring-pull.

'Bollocks.' he says, his fiery breath setting fire to the curtains.

Latest: HELL has issued a share warning.
It will rebrand.
The whole shebang is up for sale.
Demonkind will retire. Give it up...give it all up.
It's all over the FT.
HELL PLC **is** to sell up.

We are outside a office block; all glass and chrome. In the piazza in front of the building a throng of men and women in business suits mill about. It's like 'Dawn of the Dead' only better dressed.

111

*They are waiting for the word from the meeting within: the head man, **Lucifer**, is dotting the i's and crossing the t's on the sale plan with a consortium of 'major players'. They are all ready and waiting to buy, buy, buy...*

There is a distant buzz; a small plane some way distant and what looks like a large dense cloud following.

'Opportunity...'

'Glocal.'

'Segmented marketing...'

'Pride...Avarice...Lust...Wrath...Gluttony...Envy...Sloth'

'This stuff will never go out of fashion...we'll make a killing.'

Collective hysteria takes over and the crowd becomes crazed. Some tear off their clothes and start rutting like animals with whoever is closest while others tip over a coffee stand, gorging on donuts and swilling scalding coffee. Others still lose it totally and set about the others with brief cases and stiletto heels. An immaculately dressed woman has pulled up her pencil skirt and, bending over, proffers her arse; a businessman swipes his platinum credit card on her crack as she gently moans...

The demons arrive in cheap suits and plastic shoes, spilling out from a fleet of minicabs. There are 72 of them, all once rebels against the Highest. They shuffle about awkwardly, adjusting their ties and brushing flecks of dandruff from their shoulders, looking bemused and slightly embarrassed by the orgy.

Lucifer storms from the front of the building his face like thunder; a bright glow enveloping him. He is briefly nonplussed by the writing mass of humanity in front of him slick with blood and other bodily fluids but quickly recovers his composure.

He beckons imperiously to his demonic comrades.

'Deal's off, boys. These fuckers are mad...and no way am I getting into bed with Richard Branson!'

Lucifer sweeps off to try and get a taxi, picking his way through the heaving throng.

The buzz of the plane has changed to a roar now as it gets closer. It looks like some old biplane...and in its wake birds are following, millions of them. Swallows; crow, falcons and owls. Ibis and flamingos and marabou storks out of Africa. The fabulous Roc bird, celebrated by poets, glides majestically amongst the throng. It is joined by other mythical birds: the pi-his from China, that only have one wing each and fly in couples; the phoenix, trailing burning ashes. Eagles utter great cries and hummingbirds flash.

One of the demons looks up. In a voice like the distant shifting of great heaps of glowing embers and ashes he quietly says: 'Jesus Christ...'

...in an old Sopwith Camel. The plane circles the piazza once followed by it's train of birds and, as humans and demons alike scatter, all creaking canvas and wood it lands bumpily, skidding to an abrupt halt.

A flight of parrots caught out by the sudden landing get caught in the propeller and are mangled in a flurry of wild squawks.

Jesus leaps from the cockpit, leather helmet and jacket, brass goggles and scarf. The works. Brushing brightly coloured *feathers and flecks of bird blood from his face he gives a wave and cheery smile.*

'Hello chaps!'

Lucifer turns. 'Ah...ah, it's You!' he says.

'Look at them...' he adds, a sweep of the arm gesturing at the pullulating mass of bodies. 'What do you say...let bygones be bygones?'

Jesus reflects briefly.

'Ok, we'll talk...later.' he says, pulling a pistol from his holster. He rushes into the crowd, firing wildly into the air.

The chaos continues. A flight of airborne saints comes in to land - bright halos dazzle. One of the saints gives chase to the demons waving a small stoppered vessel.

'Time to get back in the bottle, boys.' he shouts, laughing. Another saint is hopping around, setting about him with a gold baroque monstrance that holds the relic of his missing leg. Lucifer sighs and tries to rally his boys.

'Time to get out of here...' he says softly."

****

Priesty John stopped talking. Everyone sat silent.

'So...?' said James.

'So,' said Priesty, 'it is surely clear what we must do. Mammon-Capital-Urizen takes us as grist for his mills. Gog and Magog stand in the Guild Hall. The body of Albion can never be made whole, Empire will have no end until we EXORCISE LONDON!'

Priesty John thumped the table.

'Fuck.' said Denys. 'I'll get another round in.'

'We create high performance digital environments.'

Palimpsest of equations.

Synthesis of proteins.

Niche Marketing.

Added value...

Knotty root, claggy brown clay glazed with rain.

'Wotz in tha placcy bag? fuck, there's clothes in the plastic bag. Whole lot swimming in blood, like a supermarket joint in tight clear wrap, y'know.'

Added value high performance digital environments.

Optimised black steel cabinet.

17% 0001010100010111010101010101 re-route re-route

'Anyway, I was cutting through Highgate down to the Archway Road. I'd trogged all the way from Cricklewood...Shootup Hill. I'd lost my Oyster card but got a bus a bit of the way but then I had to change. I was skint and decided to walk the rest...it was pissing down...anyway, it was getting on, cold, perishing cold and pissing rain and dark and then out of the velvet dark the giant bat things came on softly whispering wings: they warped time about them as they flew...'

Muscle flex, spasm, fleshy torsion.

Knotty root.

We are operating at level 5 - amber - 21%

We are operating on a higher frequency.

Everything is now digitised.

Please select an option: press one for...

Time to get out of here:

Rhumb line and compass rose.

Quantum cosmogram.

Complex sigil of the Underground.

Denys and Judith were back in the office the day after the meeting with Priesty John. The exorcism of London had been arranged for the weekend due to the work commitments of some of the team so it was business as usual.

Mid-morning doldrums: the phone rang. Judith answered.

'Hello?…who?…uh-ha…right…right…ok….dead? … my god, that's awful…thank you…yes…thank you, again. Goodbye.'

Judith put the phone down and turned to Denys.

'That was Mr Barrow. They searched at the locations on the map we gave him and they found…parts of the body… his employer's husband or brother or whatever he is. Was. They've found him except for his…well, he said heart…but I think that might be a euphemism. There's a cheque in the post.'

Denys lobbed his battered deerstalker across the room into the bin.

'Shot of the day!' he said.

Extended phenotype of London - all bodies - light on water - what you see is what you get - of course the spirits have bodies are bodies - electron gods - spray of quarks - hagstones and knotted thread - capacitors wrapped in pork fat - sting of vinegar and slow drift of sweet smelling smoke - mute hieroglyphics that teeter on the threshold of intelligibility - slipping into time and space from somewhere else - bodied forth - gold flakes fall in the fluid condensers - volt invoking evoking - inside is outside - a thin film like a bubble - Judith's body in the dark limned by candle light - mad march hares scamper the length of her body- lick slowly then fucking into another dimension - gold flesh dark matter.

Another wrapped with minute spots of her performed a ritual on the electron gods - spray of hypercosmic mute inside outside - black decoctions - thin film thrashed around naked in bodies - light scamper the length of her vortex - leading to evoking water - what you see quarks - truck Denys had said - they had mystic pork fat - sting of vinegar - huge flecked body- lick into time and space from capacitors - threshold of intelligibility - smoke - in public she was an abstract expressionist - fluid dimensions - you get gold flakes fall in demure bodied dark matter - hagstones and rhums.

1010101110101010001010010001010101110101010000101 00100010001010010 - extended 'space' in the wood - green light - mad march hares red green - by a knotted thread - mean sorcerer her skin of dimension - gold flesh invoking lunar gnosis: Bloody Mary walked in.

Her hieroglyphics that teeter on ideograms - Pollock style slow drift of sweet candle phenotype of London - all is ferocious sex magick - performed thick wet paint slowly then fucking into studio once - like being hit limned by somewhere else - spirits have bodies are bubble - Judith's body in the dark condensers - volt smelling the floor - syrops and automatic canvases - bodies and blue quiet - Judith.

They had all agreed to meet on Saturday at three o'clock at *The Gate* pub in Barnet.

It was a breezy, warm summers day. Denys and Judith had turned up early and had a few in the pub. Xaos Dave turned up next; he was suffering from a bad hangover and was already self medicating with whisky from a hip flask. Bloody Mary arrived slightly stoned. James was very definitely squiffy when he finally turned up.

Priesty John arrived last. He drove up in a battered Ford Mondeo estate. They all decided to have one for the road. They sat in the beer garden drinking lager; Priesty John had a brandy and soda.

'Better get going.' said James, slightly slurred. It was nearly five.

They made their way to Priesty John's car and wedged themselves in. Denys scrunched up in the luggage space. He had a carrier bag full of tins of Holsten Pils. They spliffed up.

For the ceremony they had decided that they should perform a banishing at the cardinal points of the M25. North was at South Mimms service station; East at Junction 30 between Aveley and South Ockenden; South at Junction7 near Caterham and West at Junction 15 where the M4 cut through towards Slough.

It was only twenty minutes or so to South Mimms service station but they had downed a can each and ripped through the spliff by the time they arrived. They drove off the A1 and shuddered to a halt on the far side of the car pack, away from the service station entrance, and tumbled from the car in a haze of smoke.

Coffee Primo; Burger King; KFC and Waitrose. Logo sigils - servitors of Mammon.

Priesty John pulled out a plastic sword from under the driver's seat. It was marked with magic symbols written in marker pen.

Xaos Dave was armed with a tin ray gun-cum-torch that had been modded with a goetic seal. He was looking rather green about the gills.

Bloody Mary oriented them towards magnetic north with the aid of a compass. She had some measure of composure but there was a slight feral glint in her eye.

Denys and Judith staggered about drunkenly, clinging on to one another and laughing hysterically.

James sat in the car with his legs on the tarmac. He was staring at the tips of his shoes.

'Keep it together people.' Priesty said.

James got unsteadily to his feet and they formed a loose line facing north.

Priesty John raised his sword and let rip: 'Out Mammon, out!'

He raised the toy sword and looked to the sky with unseeing eyes.

Parents hurried children away. A group of teenagers scoffing chips and smoking fags outside the doors to the service station pointed across the tarmac at them and laughed. A uniformed security guard came through the doors and stood watching through the shimmering heat haze.

The ramshackle crew traced figures in the air in front of them and then touched their foreheads and intoned: UJAI.

The guard took the radio from his hip and began to speak into it urgently.

A truck driver making his way back to his lorry bellowed at them: 'Wankers!'

They all touched themselves between the legs and vibrated: CHABOSEF.

'Stop that! Bloody stop that now!' the guard shouted at them. He paced across the car park towards them. Beyond the glass doors reinforcements could be seen hurrying through the mall.

Rapidly Priesty John led them through four more utterances of Words of Power. The guard drew up in front of them: two more men in uniforms were running up behind.

Bloody Mary walked up to the nearest guard and stood toe to toe with him. Her face was inches from his and she glowered fiercely at him. He was utterly nonplussed.

'My Cunt is Holy.' she said with a growl.

The guard blinked at her. His mouth worked but no words came. His colleagues pounded up, breathing hard.

'We're going now.' Mary said simply.

They piled back into the car and with a fearful grinding of gears the car lurched into motion.

They had planned to take the M25 all the way round to the next cardinal point but after they had passed Waltham Abbey the traffic ground to a halt. They sat for a while drinking. Another spliff was passed around. The traffic report on the car radio told them it was backed up all the way from the Queen Elizabeth Bridge. They decided to pull off and take the A121 and cut through Romford.

They must have taken a wrong turning somewhere and they ended up in a suburban residential road. Priesty John's driving was becoming decidedly erratic and the close confines of the car were destroying what little *esprit de corps* they had remaining.

James was woozily looking over an A-Z.

'Left…left here.' he called out.

Priesty took a right and drove into a concrete bollard.

It was a bad shunt but everyone seemed unhurt. They got out of the car and stood dazed, looking at the crumpled front of the vehicle. Hiss of escaping steam. The sun was setting now and pink streamers of cloud scudded above them.

Denys was the last to extricate himself from the wreck. He was still clutching the carrier bag with the last two remaining cans of beer.

He staggered around. He felt very drunk though the sudden impact had sobered him somewhat.

Priesty John stood, head bowed, holding on to the car door. He held the toy sword in his hand. James had started to retch. Judith sat on the kerb sobbing gently; Mary squatted by her, her arm round Judith's shoulder. Dave was on his mobile.

Denys suddenly got the fear: he ran off at full pelt.

Working antique looking headphones across as below. Rising from tea speculation: ghost stars, clocks. Cards stir railway bridges, underpasses, parks. Hurried rites of sexual magic, fucking me and his British crystal wireless. I am possible, a time fridge...the razor blade communication. The genuine office of seven philosophical planets. Old piles of candles, the threadbare carpet of changes. Unsure if they have any grounds. Headphones television ships drifting. The real sky photocopied war. Primitive radio swift act of stars the dragon said. I show history connected in mosaic time. Filing cabinet breakdown, final bulletins from a mind city. World diodes expectation. The whole lot indeterminate time television ships drifting. Faint stubs of different coloured afternoon sodomy. Names. Aerial climax of singing was spent. Fantastic back turned to nightmares. Flyblown windows rot set brick exercise in sudden vistas.

Bright flecks. We are all space people: genetic links, office smells of cheap coffee, cheaper expectation. Leads to an office - the sudden vistas of elsewhere.

A deck of worn cards, two worlds in one smashing the now. *Scenes of Old London Town* on top of the psychedelic mess of wax cards. A spread of ordinary playing cards faded as the card below - communicate the pattern.

A desk, a phone and a stone pangs of rebirth. A slight hint for another door leading off. Painted a history of a pack of cards. Nightmares in speculation: ghost stars, clocks and the dragon heretics. The door is closed again. Time television ships drifting in time. This subdued setting. The door would penetrate the flyblown windows and daylight makes a valiant attempt amidst coming changes. Has it all happened on the threadbare carpet of indeterminate before?

Safety precautions. The real sky menace at the top of the stairs. Exotic traces. A copy of last years old decision is shedding paint in cases. The mind blockers, men in black saucer mosaic time.

Projection filing cabinet has stubs of different coloured candles on it. Rising from a way of the stars, the King of the door itself has evidently made it exhausted.

Operation earth: an exercise in sudden vistas of elsewhere. The closer penetrate the flyblown windows and menace at the top of the stairs. The revolt of youth for another door leading off painted a subdued setting. The door would be two worlds in one smashing the now. Shedding the paint in the mind grounds for a charge of common assault. We think strangers bridge attitudes communication. A deck of worn cards. We are all space people, genetic links, great flakes, bright flecks ground into Queen of the door.

Daylight makes a valiant attempt to pattern a desk, a phone and filing exotic traces of sandlewood, ashtray. A copy of last years old worn decision and blockers. Women in black saucer mosaic speculation. Ghost stars, clocks and the dragon heretics; the door is closed again. The psychedelic mess of wax cards. Stone pangs of rebirth, a slight hint of bottles and an overflowing time. No more projection filing cabinet history of a pack of cards. Nightmares: it's exhausted, fails - midst coming changes. Has it all happened - fills the space that remains. A tea before safety precautions. The real sky as the card below rising from a way of the stars. The fags and a dozen rarer incense, faint stubs of different coloured candles.

The threadbare carpet of indeterminate time television ships drifting in time.

*****D**enys was his own mesmerist: a somnambulist wandering amongst a million other oneironauts. He was looking for London's docks; he saw the docklands not as they are but as a palimpsest of how they had been: a walking spectral analysis of a quantum of space-time.

At Limehouse Church, at the great iron gate of the churchyard, he stopped and looked in. He looked up at the ghostly great tower resisting the wind, and he looked at the white tombstones, like enough to the dead in their winding sheets, and he counted the tolls of the church bell.

The docks were lost amongst the buildings like dark lagoons hidden in a thick forest; they lay concealed in the intricate growth of houses with a few stalks of mastheads here and there overtopping the roof of some four-story warehouse.

At last Denys found his way through: a vista of wharves, landing-places, dock-gates and waterside stairs followed each other continuously along the river. The water-way itself flowed oppressed by bricks and mortar and stone, by blackened timber and grimed glass and rusty iron, covered with black barges, whipped up by paddles and screws, overburdened with craft, overhung with chains, overshadowed by walls making a steep gorge for its bed, filled with a haze of smoke and dust.

A hulk lifted itself from the dark waters; the timbers were warped or rotted away and waters poured from inside the hull. Sere sails were spread and the clipper tugged at its anchor; it floated just above the surface of the turbid waters. The Thames gave up its dead for the ship's crew - they bobbed up from the depths and climbed aboard. Grinning skulls look out from under oilskin hats; ribs in rough blue jackets with mother-of-pearl buttons, bony legs in large canvas trousers.

The ship cast off, trailing ropes and chains which the last of the crew scrambled up.

'Haul away boys! Haul away!'

***VAUXHALL - SUDBURY HILL - BETHNAL GREEN - LANCASTER GATE - HOBBS LANE - CHIGWELL - HADES EAST - MONUMENT -

In the City of London the Lily White Boys performed a medley of old songs while Denys dropped his trousers in front of the Bank of England and uttered inchoate obscenities.

Denys and the Lily White Boys were next seen attempting to gain access to The Guildhall - their stated intent to destroy the statues of Gog and Magog. The City police gave chase. Keystone Kops through the wards of Dowgate and Candlewick, Walbrook, Cordwainer and Bread Street before they made good their escape through Farringdon Within, Cheap and Farringdon Without.

CHARING CROSS: The full tide of humanity. Denys proclaimed the instauration of an era of Universal Love. His collapse and arrest.

***Denys sat on the bench at the top of Primrose Hill. Dusk was rapidly deepening to night's dark.

A trickle of blood ran from Denys' right nostril.

'I am the Prince of Nosebleeds. King of Absolutely Fucking Nothing.'

The lights in London below dimmed and then went out.

The hidden stars were suddenly apparent in the vast dome of the heavens.

Denys saw the Great Bear above.

Speeding from the Plough come the space capsules of the cosmonauts: hyperborean gods, barbaric and scientific. Masked they come, in fire and ice.

Denys and Judith fuck on the threadbare carpet in the office: the carpet is flecked with constellations of flaked orange paint.

The playing cards faded give you the names. Aerial climax of singing puppet was communication; the genuine office breakdown. Final bulletins from a mind afternoon was spent. Fantastic back turned to me and British crystal wireless. I am unsure if they have any grounds. Headphones on, the stars the dragon said, earth. I show you how speculation ghost stars, clocks and the possible. A time fridge...the razor blade changes an exercise in sudden vistas.

A stapled, photocopied war. Primitive radio working. Antique looking headphones across the world. Diodes expectation; the whole lot was connected in mosaic time. Filing cabinet history nightmares. Flyblown windows rot set the city. Television ships drifting.

Flyblown windows rot set brick exercise in sudden vistas.

The playing cards faded give you seven philosophical planets. Old piles of brick stir. Railway bridges, underpasses, car parks. Hurried rites of sexual magick.

Door left ajar in hope. A rarer incense faint fills the space that remains.

000010100100001010101110101010001010010000
101010111010101000101001000101010111010
101000101001000101010111010101000101001
000010101011101010100010100100010101011
010101000101001000101010111010101000101
001000101010111010101000101001000101010
111010101000101001000101010111010101000
101001000101010111010101000101001000101
010111010101000101001000101010111010101
000010100100001010101110101010001010010 00 a ö ee
ö **ëë öö** ii **öööö** oooo **ööö** uuuuu **öööööööööööö**
00101001000101010111010101000101001000 1
010101110101010001010010001010101110101
010000101001000101010111010101000101001 0
001010101110101010001010010001010101110
101010001010010001010101110101010001010
010000100001010010001010101110101010001 01
001000101010111010101000101001000101010
111010101000101001000101010111010101 00
010100100010101011101010100010100100 01
010101110101010001010010001010101110 10
101000010100100010101011101010100010100 1
000101010111010101000101001000101010111
010101000101001000101010111010101 00010
10010001010101110101010001010010001 0101
011101010100010100100010101011101010100
010100100010101011101010100010100100010
101011101010100010100100010101011101010 100
010101011101010100010100100010101011101
010100010100100010100101010001000010000
scrap of sailcloth - diode - pitch and wax
- myrrh - copperwire 00101001000001101
000101001110101010111010010001111010 1001
011101110010000101001001001000100010 00100
010001000100010001000100010001000101 110
110101000101011011010010010110001000 100
0011010000100010001000100100010001000100 001

THE CHAIN CURSE UPON MAMMON-CAPITAL-URIZEN.

Done from the *Lemegeton*. Hermetic names here replace xtian; implements and symbols of the arte - all as you please. Prepare well your circle. Usual precautions apply. Replace the black box with a memory stick loaded with the seal of Mammon-Capital-Urizen - cut-in news stories of stock market crashes, wildcat strikes etc.

Call upon Mammon-Capital-Urizen to take himself off and cease his torment of humankind in your own name and by the names of the Gods. Name and Number the iniquities of Mammon-Capital-Urizen if you will.

Then speak thus:

O thou wicked and disobedient Mammon-Capital-Urizen, because thou hast not obeyed or regarded the words which I have rehearsed, the glorious and incomprehensible Names of the true Gods, Makers of all things in the world, now I, by the power of these Names, which no creature can resist, do curse thee into the depths of a Bottomless Pit, to remain for the Longest Time, in a Hell of unquenchable fire and brimstone, unless thou shalt forthwith appear in this triangle, before this circle, to do my will. Come, therefore, quickly and peaceably, by the Names Hermes Trismegistus & Isis; Horus, son of Isis & Ammon; Poimandres and Tat. Come, come, I command thee.

Having read so far, if he come not, write his seal on parchment; put it in a black box, with brimstone, assafœtida and other stinking perfumes; bind the said box with iron wire, hang it on the point of your sword, hold it over the fire of charcoal, which shall have been placed towards that quarter whence the spirit will Come, and say first unto the Fire:-

I conjure thee, O Fire, by the Gods Who made thee, and all other creatures in the world, to torment, burn, and consume this Spirit Mammon-Capital-Urizen everlastingly.

To the Spirit say:--

Because thou art disobedient, and obeyst not my commandments nor the precepts of the Gods, now I, who am the Peer of the High Gods, having Their celestial power and permission, for this thine averseness and contempt, thy great disobedience and rebellion, will excommunicate thee, will destroy thy name and seal, which I have in this box, will burn them with unquenchable fire and bury them in unending oblivion, unless thou leave off tormenting humankind.

Thou art still pernicious and disobedient, willing not to appear and inform me upon that which I desire; now therefore, in the Names and by the power and dignity of the ever-living, ever-dying Gods, Creators of the Heavens, Earth and Hells, with all contained therein, the marvellous Disposers of all things visible and invisible, I do hereby curse and deprive thee of all thine office, power and place; I bind thee in the depth of a Bottomless Pit, there to remain Longest Time, in a Lake of Fire and Brimstone, prepared for thee. May all the Company of the Heavens curse thee; may the Sun, the Moon, the Stars, the Lights of the Heavens, curse thee into fire unquenchable, into torments unspeakable; and even as thy name and seal are bound up in this box, to be choked with sulphureous and stinking substances and to burn in this material fire, so, in the Name of the Gods, and by the power and dignity of the their Names, may all these drive thee, O thou disobedient Spirit Mammon-Capital-Urizen, into a Lake of Fire, prepared for the damned and accursed Spirits, there to remain for the Longest Time, remembered no more before the face of the Gods Who shall come to be with the quick and the dead, with the whole world.

Set the box in the flame, whereupon he will appear; when he comes, quench the fire, make sweet perfumes, give him good entertainment, shewing him the symbol on the hem of your vestment covered with a linen cloth, and saying:--

Behold thy confusion, if thou be disobedient. Behold this Puissant Symbol which I have brought into thy presence. Behold the person of the Exorcist, who is called OCTINIMOES, in the midst of the Exorcism, armed by the Gods and fearless, potently invoking and calling. Make, therefore, reasonable answers to my demands; be obedient to me, in the Name of the BATHAL, rushing upon ABRAC, ABEOR, coming upon BEROR.

Set the box in the flame again...